# THE
# LEGO®
## FAN'S GUIDE

**For DK**

Editors Pamela Afram, Ruth Amos, Jo Casey, Hannah Dolan, Alastair Dougall, Laura Gilbert, Emma Grange, Matt Jones, Lindsay Kent, Shari Last, Julia March, Helen Murray, Catherine Saunders, Lisa Stock, Victoria Taylor

Designers Neha Ahuja, Owen Bennett, Jill Bunyan, Jon Hall, Guy Harvey, Nathan Martin, Lynne Moulding, Robert Perry, Mark Richards, Sam Richiardi, Lauren Rosier, Anamica Roy, Clive Savage, Anne Sharples, Rajdeep Singh, Chitrak Srivastava, Lisa Sodeau, Rhys Thomas, Toby Truphet

Senior Editor Tori Kosara

Senior DTP Designer David McDonald

Senior Producer Katherine Whyte

Managing Editor Simon Hugo

Design Manager Ron Stobbart

Creative Manager Sarah Harland

Art Director Lisa Lanzarini

Publisher Julie Ferris

Publishing Director Simon Beecroft

Content produced in association with
**Tall Tree**

This edition published in 2014
Content first published as *The LEGO® MOVIE: The Essential Guide* (2014), LEGO® *Play Book* (2013), LEGO® *Minifigure Year by Year: A Visual History* (2013), *The LEGO® Ideas Book* (2011), *The LEGO® Book* (2009), *Standing Small* (2009), by Dorling Kindersley Limited, 80 Strand, London WC2R 0RL
A Penguin Random House Company

ISBN: 978-0-2411-8814-9

Printed and bound by TBB, a.s. in Slovakia.

www.dk.com
www.LEGO.com

A WORLD OF IDEAS:
**SEE ALL THERE IS TO KNOW**

# CONTENTS

# THE
# LEGO®
## FAN'S GUIDE

# "Only the Best…"

**"ONLY THE BEST IS GOOD ENOUGH."** That was the motto of LEGO Group founder Ole Kirk Kristiansen, and he believed in it so strongly that his son Godtfred Kirk Christiansen carved it on a sign and hung it on his father's carpentry workshop's wall. Ole Kirk believed that children deserved to have toys made with the highest quality materials and workmanship, and he was determined that the toys manufactured in his workshop would last and remain just as fun through years of play. Today, the words of the company's founder remain its driving force, and LEGO® products continue to be passed down from one generation to the next, sparking the creativity and imaginations of millions of children and adults all over the world ●

# DET·BEDSTE·ER IKKE·FOR·GODT

**Carved in wood** as a reminder to his employees to never skimp on quality, Ole Kirk's motto has been a guiding principle for the LEGO Group for more than 75 years.

**Workers** pose for a photograph, taken in the late 1940s. Above their heads, Ole Kirk's motto is proudly displayed upon the workshop wall.

# A Family Business

**THROUGH THREE** generations of family ownership and family management, the LEGO Group has grown from a small local company into one of the world´s leading providers of creative, developmental play products. Each generation has contributed to the LEGO® brand's expansion and continued success ●

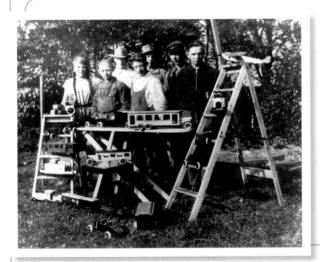

Ole Kirk Kristiansen recreates the patterns for the wooden LEGO duck in 1943 after a fire the previous year destroyed the LEGO workshop and all of the company's designs.

Workers pose with a range of the first wooden toys in 1932. "It was not until the day that I said to myself, you must choose between your carpentry and the toys that things started to make sense," Ole Kirk recalled.

## AN IMAGE OF HOPE

The year 1932 was a difficult one for company founder Ole Kirk Kristiansen, combining Europe's economic depression, looming bankruptcy and deep personal loss at the death of his wife. While bringing up four young sons on his own, Ole Kirk created a new business: making wooden toys. The years that followed were little easier, often forcing him to borrow money from his family to keep his workshop afloat and maintain his standards for creating the finest possible wooden toys.

This wooden plane is a reconstruction of the one on top of the ladder in the photograph on the left. Today, it symbolises the company's ability to rise above adversity.

## CHILDREN DESERVE THE BEST

The company's toys needed to work and work well, even in the hands of the most enthusiastically active child. From the very start, Ole Kirk was dedicated to quality. He worked under the self-coined motto "Only the best is good enough," and his sons and employees were often reminded that "This is the way we do things" at the LEGO workshop. By choosing a name contracted from "LEg GOdt," or "Play Well" in Danish, Ole Kirk emphasised that the LEGO name needed to represent a standard of quality that would set the company apart from its competitors.

Godtfred Kirk Christiansen (GKC) continued his father's philosophy when, under his leadership, the company changed to concentrate on the new LEGO System of Play in 1955. The need to constantly improve product quality led him to develop the LEGO brick's unique "clutch" principle, and better materials and production technology maintained its precise shape. Godtfred Kirk was a firm believer in the LEGO code of "good play," and in 1963, he introduced the "10 important characteristics" for future LEGO product development.

## GKC's Watchwords for the LEGO System

- Unlimited play possibilities
- For girls, for boys
- Enthusiasm for all ages
- Play all year round
- Healthy and quiet play
- Endless hours of play
- Imagination, creativity, development
- Each new product multiplies the play value of the rest
- Always topical
- Safety and quality

**Ole Kirk Kristiansen,** Godtfred Kirk Christiansen, and Kjeld Kirk Kristiansen at Ole Kirk's 60th birthday party in 1951. Three generations building on each other's achievements!

**From early on,** Kjeld Kirk Kristiansen realised the potential of LEGO bricks and built his own models, some of which became official sets. Here, Kjeld and his father discuss one of Kjeld's models in 1978.

> "Children mean everything to us. Children and their development. And this must pervade everything we do."
>
> Kjeld Kirk Kristiansen, 1996

### FOCUS ON CHILDREN

Third-generation company owner Kjeld Kirk Kristiansen created a "system within the system" with his own model for product development, establishing a division to provide each age group of customers with the right toys at the right time in their lives. Kjeld Kirk Kristiansen believed strongly in the LEGO brand and became a driving force to change the consumer's perception of it from just a great construction toy to a world-recognised icon of quality, creativity and learning. In 1996 he explained: "My grandfather's main drive was the perfection of quality craftsmanship. My father's main focus was on our unique product idea with all its inherent possibilities. I see myself as a more globally oriented leader, seeking to fully exploit our brand potential for further developing and broadening our product range and business concept, based upon our product idea and brand values."

Launched in 1932 as one of the workshop's first wooden toys, the yo-yo enjoyed a brief period of great popularity. When the craze and sales declined, the remaining stock was recycled into wheels for other toys, like the pull-along pony and trap below.

Pony and Trap (1937)

# Wooden Toys

**THE STORY** of one of the world's most successful toy companies began in 1916 when Danish master carpenter Ole Kirk Kristiansen bought a workshop in the little town of Billund and set up a business building houses and furniture. In 1932, with the worldwide Great Depression threatening to close his carpentry shop for good, Ole Kirk turned his skills to creating a range of toys for children. These beautifully made and painted playthings included yo-yos, wooden blocks, pull-along animals and vehicles of all kinds ●

## PULL-ALONG TOYS

During the 1930s and 1940s, the company had great success with its wide range of pull-along wooden toy animals for young children. Produced in several different colour schemes, this rolling duck, painted to resemble a male mallard, was one of the most popular early LEGO toys.

### WOODEN BLOCKS

Decorated with colourful painted letters and numbers, LEGO wooden blocks could be stacked and arranged into words to help young children learn the alphabet and spelling. Forerunners of the plastic brick (which appeared in 1949), these blocks date from 1946.

Duck (1935)

Beak opens and shuts as wheels turn

"Clumsy Hans" (1936)

### "CLUMSY HANS"

From the popular "Klods-Hans" fairy tale by Danish writer and poet Hans Christian Andersen, Clumsy Hans bobs up and down on his billy goat as you pull this toy along.

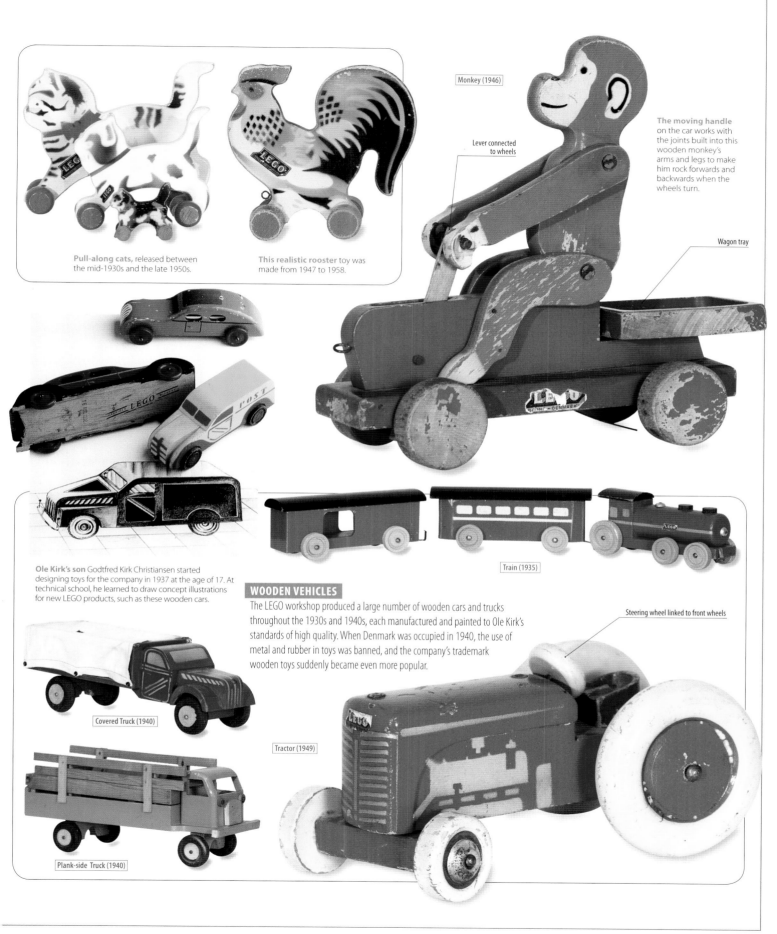

Monkey (1946)

Lever connected to wheels

**The moving handle** on the car works with the joints built into this wooden monkey's arms and legs to make him rock forwards and backwards when the wheels turn.

Wagon tray

**Pull-along cats**, released between the mid-1930s and the late 1950s.

**This realistic rooster** toy was made from 1947 to 1958.

Train (1935)

**Ole Kirk's son** Godtfred Kirk Christiansen started designing toys for the company in 1937 at the age of 17. At technical school, he learned to draw concept illustrations for new LEGO products, such as these wooden cars.

## WOODEN VEHICLES

The LEGO workshop produced a large number of wooden cars and trucks throughout the 1930s and 1940s, each manufactured and painted to Ole Kirk's standards of high quality. When Denmark was occupied in 1940, the use of metal and rubber in toys was banned, and the company's trademark wooden toys suddenly became even more popular.

Steering wheel linked to front wheels

Covered Truck (1940)

Tractor (1949)

Plank-side Truck (1940)

# Plastic Toys

**IN 1947,** Ole Kirk purchased a plastic injection-moulding machine imported from Britain. One of the first in Denmark, the machine cost DKK 30,000, one-15th of the company's entire earnings for the year. Plastic toys were expensive to manufacture, but the risk paid off: by 1951, half of the company's toys were made from plastic ●

**One of the company's** first plastic toys was a baby's rattle shaped like a fish. Blending different plastic colours inside the moulding machine gave it an eye-catching marbled appearance.

LEGO Mursten (1953 )

The slits in the bricks enabled builders to insert windows and doors.

The boy in the white shirt is Ole Kirk's grandson, Kjeld Kirk Kristiansen; the girl is his sister.

## BIRTH OF A BRICK

The first LEGO® bricks were produced in 1949 under the name "Automatic Binding Bricks." At first, they were just a handful out of about 200 plastic and wooden toys the company manufactured. Made from cellulose acetate, they resembled today's bricks but had slits on their sides and were completely hollow underneath, without tubes to lock them together. In 1953, they were renamed LEGO Mursten ("LEGO Bricks").

## CARS AND TRUCKS

A new series of realistic plastic cars based on real auto models started in 1958 with the launch of the company-wide LEGO System of Play. Designed to complement the new Town Plan sets, many of the vehicles included bases and display containers with studs for attaching LEGO bricks.

262 Opel Rekord with Garage (1961)

**This plastic car** came in a transparent display case with an opening door and LEGO System studs on top.

260 VW Beetle (1958)

**Produced** in various colours and sizes between 1957 and 1967, the VW Beetle could also be purchased with a showcase box that included a LEGO brick VW logo plate.

## CARS AND TRUCKS

With the new plastics technology came the ability to design and produce toys with much greater detail and accuracy than ever before. Colourful cars and trucks were a popular product among children, who could collect and play with all the latest models and styles.

**Colourful artwork** decorates the box of this 1950s Chevrolet truck collection.

**Many toys** combined plastic with other materials. This Esso fuel truck had a plastic cab and a painted wooden trailer.

The real Ferguson Model TE20 tractor (nicknamed the "Little Grey Fergie"), illustrated here on the toy's new 1953 packaging, was manufactured from 1946 to 1956.

**Just like the real thing,** the LEGO Ferguson Tractor was designed to pull a variety of farming attachments.

**Originally** sold fully assembled, the tractor was released again in 1953 with the option of putting it together yourself.

## FERGUSON TRACTOR (1952)

One of the company's biggest early successes in plastic toys was the Ferguson Tractor. Its highly-detailed plastic-injection mould cost as much to make as the price of a real tractor, but with 75,000 pieces sold in its first year alone, the gamble quickly paid off. The increasing popularity of industrialised farming in Europe meant that the Ferguson Tractor arrived during a time when more and more farmers were switching from horses to tractors, making it a must-have toy for the 1950s child. The profits that the toy tractor earned made it possible for the company to invest in its still new and unproven plastic bricks.

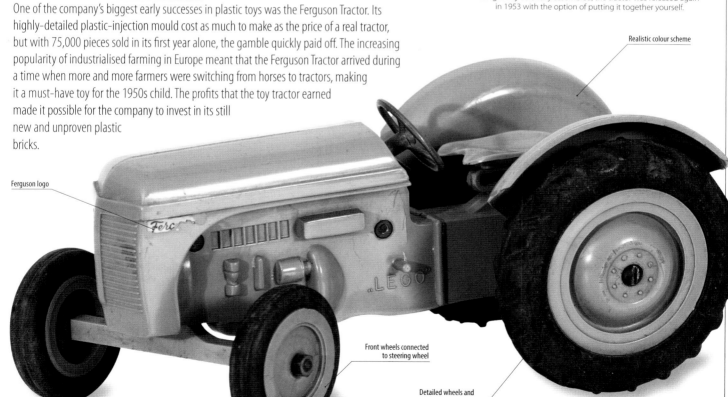

Realistic colour scheme

Ferguson logo

Front wheels connected to steering wheel

Detailed wheels and rubber tyres

# Work Hard, Play Well

**THE LEGO GROUP** has been making its famous bricks for over half a century, but its story doesn't begin there. Presented here is a timeline of the company's earliest days, from the birth of its founder, to its humble beginnings in a carpentry workshop in the Danish village of Billund, the move to producing wooden and then plastic toys, the birth of the first LEGO® bricks and the dawn of the revolutionary LEGO System of Play ●

Ole Kirk aged 20 years old.

### 1891
● Ole Kirk, founder of the LEGO Group, is born at Omvrå near Filskov, not far from the village of Billund in Denmark.

Ole Kirk's 1936 motto for the company.

### 1935
● The business manufactures the first LEGO wooden duck, and markets "Kirk's Sandgame," its first construction toy.

### 1936
● Ole Kirk coins the company motto, "Only the best is good enough." His son Godtfred Kirk Christiansen carves Ole Kirk´s motto and hangs it on the workshop wall.

### 1937
● Godtfred Kirk Christiansen begins designing models for the company at the age of 17.

### 1939
● The LEGO factory hires its 10th employee.

### 1942
● A fire destroys the factory and Ole Kirk's life's work. A new toy factory is built, and he remakes all of the lost designs himself.

### 1950
● On his 30th birthday, Godtfred Kirk Christiansen is appointed Junior Managing Director of the company.

### 1952
● The LEGO Ferguson tractor is released.
● A building base with 10 x 20 studs is sold for use with the interlocking bricks.

### 1952
● A new LEGO manufacturing plant is built at the cost of DKK 350,000.

### 1953
● "Automatic Binding Bricks" are renamed "LEGO Bricks" ("LEGO Mursten" in Danish). The LEGO name is moulded onto every brick.

Some of Ole Kirk's tools.

LEGO

## 1916
● Ole Kirk buys the Billund Joinery Manufacturing and Carpentry Workshop and sets up business as a self-employed carpenter and joiner.

## 1924
● Ole Kirk's three sons play with matches and the workshop burns down! He builds a larger one, renting out the remaining space.

## 1932
● Ole Kirk starts to manufacture and sell wooden toys.

## 1934
● Ole Kirk holds a competition among his employees to name the company, with a bottle of wine as the prize. He wins it himself with the name "LEGO," short for "LEg GOdt," or "Play Well" in Danish. Coincidentally, the word can also mean "I put together" in Latin.

Illustrations of animals and people added more possibilities.

The first bricks have no logo

## 1943
● The company gains its 43rd employee.

## 1946
● New LEGO products include wooden blocks with painted letters and numbers.

## 1947
● Ole Kirk imports a plastic injection-moulding machine from the UK.
● The company produces its first plastic toys, including a ball for infants and Monopoli, an educational road safety game.

## 1948
● The firm now employs 50 people.
● New products include a pinball game.

## 1949
● "Automatic Binding Bricks," the company's first plastic interlocking bricks, are produced. The company now makes about 200 plastic and wooden toys, including a new plastic fish and sailor.

## 1954
● The name "LEGO" is officially registered in Denmark.
● The first brick-compatible LEGO window and door elements are produced.
● Godtfred Kirk Christiansen has the idea of creating a LEGO System of Play based around the amazingly versatile LEGO brick.

## 1955
● The System of Play is launched with the release of the Town Plan range of 28 construction sets and eight vehicles.

# The LEGO® System of Play

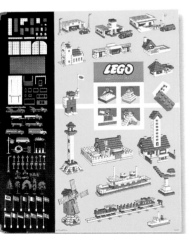

**The first LEGO System set** was "Town Plan No. 1." Appearing on its packaging was young Kjeld Kirk Kristiansen, son of GKC and the grandson of company founder Ole Kirk Kristiansen.

**1954 WAS A YEAR** in which Godtfred Kirk Christiansen (GKC) did a lot of thinking about the future of the LEGO Group. Returning from a toy fair in Britain, he got talking to a colleague, who pointed out that there was no *system* in the toy industry. That was all the inspiration GKC needed. He decided to create a structured system of products. Reviewing all the toys made by the company, he saw that the LEGO® brick was the best choice for this project. The LEGO System of Play launched the following year with the Town Plan range of construction sets ●

Of the System of Play, GKC wrote: "Our idea is to create a toy that prepares the child for life, appeals to the imagination and develops the creative urge and joy of creation that are the driving force in every human being."

Town Plan No.1 (1955)

Additional Town Plan boards were sold separately

## TOWN PLAN

The original Town Plan No. 1 set included everything children needed to assemble their own realistic town centres, from a colourful street board to citizens, cars and trucks and lots of red, white and blue LEGO bricks. The first street boards were soft plastic; they were changed to wooden fibreboard in 1956.

## A GROWING SYSTEM

The idea behind the LEGO System was that every element should connect to every other element; the more bricks, the more building possibilities. With Town Plan, children could make their towns bigger and better with each new set, and thanks to the included extra building ideas (pictured below left), they could make more than just what was pictured on the box.

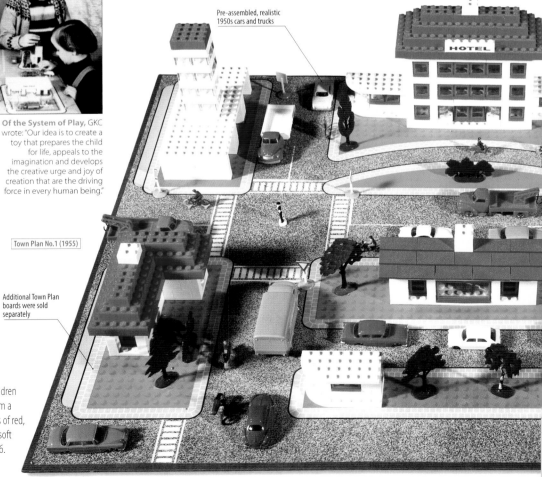

Pre-assembled, realistic 1950s cars and trucks

## A NEW TOWN PLAN

In 2008, the company celebrated the 50th anniversary of the patenting of the modern LEGO brick with a new version of the classic Town Plan set. The special-edition set let kids and collectors create a town centre from the 1950s, with a movie theater, petrol station and town hall.

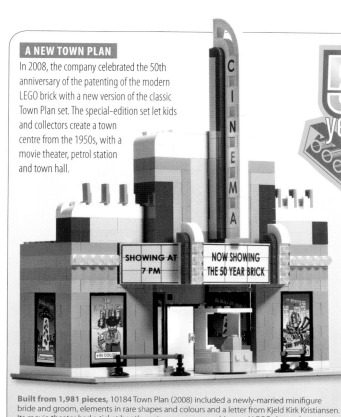

**In honour** of the LEGO brick's golden anniversary, the set included three metallic gold bricks built into the town's central fountain.

**Kjeld Kirk Kristiansen,** now the owner of the company, reprised his childhood starring role by appearing on the new Town Plan set's packaging.

**Built from 1,981 pieces,** 10184 Town Plan (2008) included a newly-married minifigure bride and groom, elements in rare shapes and colours and a letter from Kjeld Kirk Kristiansen. Its movie theater had a ticket booth, seats, a popcorn machine and LEGO themed posters.

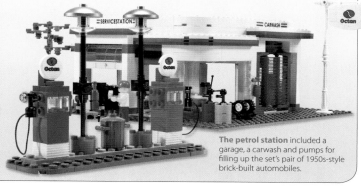

**The petrol station** included a garage, a carwash and pumps for filling up the set's pair of 1950s-style brick-built automobiles.

Detailed traffic signs

Painted crossing guards directed traffic

Esso petrol station

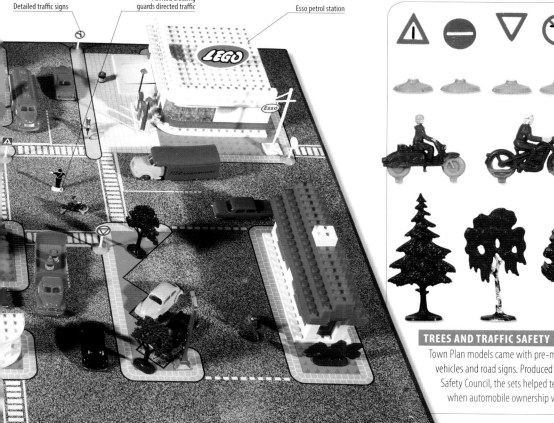

## TREES AND TRAFFIC SAFETY

Town Plan models came with pre-moulded and painted trees, people, vehicles and road signs. Produced in collaboration with the Danish Road Safety Council, the sets helped teach traffic safety to children in an era when automobile ownership was steeply on the rise.

# A Worldwide System

**THANKS TO THE NEW** LEGO® System of Play, the company was no longer just another toy manufacturer. It now had a unique brand identity all its own and a mission to bring its message of creative fun to the rest of the world. It wasn't easy to convince the first few international markets to gamble on importing plastic bricks, but by the end of the 1960s, the LEGO name was known in every household, with sets for preschoolers and even its very own theme park ●

## 1956
● The first foreign sales company, LEGO Spielwaren GmbH, is founded in Hohenweststedt in Germany.

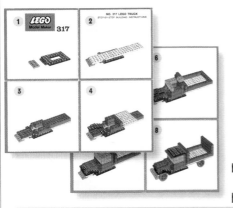

Fire destroys the wooden toy stock.

Production concentrates on plastic products.

## 1958
● Ole Kirk passes away and Godtfred Kirk Christiansen becomes head of the company.
● The company now has 140 employees.
● The first sloping roof-tile bricks are produced.

## 1959
● The LEGO Futura department is established to conceive, plan and oversee the design of new LEGO sets.
● LEGO divisions are founded in France, the UK, Belgium and Sweden.
● New products include BILOfix wood and plastic construction toys.

## 1960
● A fire destroys the workshop where the company's wooden toys are made. A decision is made to stop making wooden toys and focus entirely on the LEGO System.
● LEGO divisions are established in Finland and the Netherlands. Approximately 400 employees now work at the company headquarters in Billund.

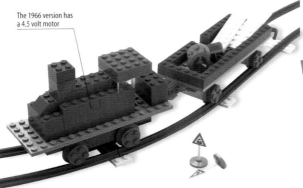

The 1966 version has a 4.5 volt motor

Just one of 1967's millions of LEGO sets.

## 1964
● LEGO model sets with building instructions are produced.
● LEGO products are sold in the Middle East.
● LEGO bricks are exhibited at the Danish pavilion of the New York World Fair.
● The Ole Kirk Foundation is established to help support the arts and other cultural activities.

## 1965
● LEGO product sales start in Spain.
● The company now has more than 600 employees.

## 1966
● The first battery-powered LEGO Train sets are launched.
● LEGO products are now sold in 42 countries.
● The first official LEGO Club begins in Canada.

## 1967
● More than 18 million LEGO sets are sold during the year.
● The LEGO® DUPLO® building system is patented in August.
● There are now 218 different LEGO element shapes.
● A LEGO Club is founded in Sweden.

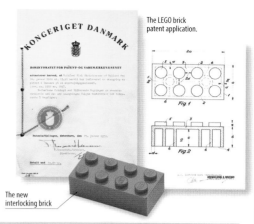

The LEGO brick patent application.

The new interlocking brick

## 1957
- The LEGO Group celebrates its Silver Jubilee.
- New products include bricks with light-bulbs and VW Beetles in eight colours.

## 1957
- The LEGO brick is updated with a new stud-and-tube interlocking system that increases building possibilities and improves model stability.

## 1958
- The LEGO brick's interlocking principle is patented at 1:58 pm on 28 January.

The launch of LEGO bricks in the US.

The LEGO aeroplane at Billund Airstrip.

## 1961
- The design for a LEGO wheel is discovered in a product developer's drawer. Wheels are released the next year, letting children build rolling vehicles of all kinds.

## 1961
- Godtfred Kirk Christiansen buys a small aeroplane, and a landing field is built outside Billund.
- LEGO sales begin in the US and Canada through a licence agreement with the Samsonite Corp. luggage company.
- The first LEGO preschool lines are launched: Terapi I, II and III.
- LEGO Italy is established.

## 1962
- LEGO products are first sold in Singapore, Hong Kong, Australia, Morocco and Japan.
- LEGO Australia is established.

## 1963
- ABS (acrylonitrile butadiene styrene) replaces cellulose acetate as the material used to make LEGO bricks. It is more colour-fast and allows better moulding.
- Billund airport officially opens.
- LEGO Austria is established.

LEGO DUPLO bricks were eight times the size of original bricks.

## 1968
- The first LEGOLAND® park opens in Billund on June 7th. 625,000 people visit in the first year.
- LEGO DUPLO bricks are test-marketed in Sweden.

## 1969
- The LEGO DUPLO range for children under five years old is launched internationally.
- A 12-volt motor is added to the LEGO Train series.

# Bricks for Everyone

**THE 1970s** saw LEGO® products branch out in new ways. Creating construction toys that girls, boys and experienced builders of all ages would enjoy became a key goal, and all of the company's products and brands were brought together under an iconic new logo. LEGO people appeared for the first time, leading up to the minifigures that LEGO fans know today, and the classic LEGO Play Themes were born ●

## 1970
- The company now has almost 1,000 employees in Billund.
- Small car sets are sold at pocket-money prices.

US Presidents Washington, Jefferson, Roosevelt and Lincoln

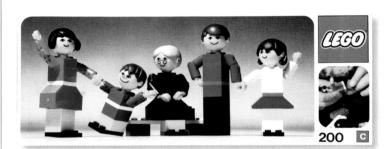

## 1974
- The first LEGO people are released, with round heads, movable arms and bodies built from bricks.
- The best-selling #200 LEGO Family set included a father, mother, son, daughter and grandmother.

## 1974
- A brick replica of Mount Rushmore is constructed in LEGOLAND® Billund by Danish artist Bjørn Richter.
- The park receives its 5 millionth visitor.
- LEGO Spain is established.

## 1978
- The first three LEGO Play Themes are introduced.
- The LEGO Castle theme features medieval knights and castles.

## 1978
- The first modern-style minifigures with printed faces and movable arms and legs appear.
- The LEGO Town theme lets children build modern buildings and vehicles.
- LEGO baseplates with road markings are produced.

## 1978
- The LEGO Space theme lets builders' imaginations run wild with outer space adventures.
- A LEGO Club is founded in the UK with a magazine titled *Bricks 'n' Pieces*.
- LEGO Japan is established.

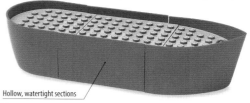

The tugboat was one of the first floating LEGO ships.

Hollow, watertight sections

## 1971
- LEGO sets for girls are launched, including dolls' houses and furniture.

## 1972
- 1.8 billion LEGO bricks and other elements have been produced.

## 1973
- A new LEGO logo unifies all of the company's products

## 1973
- The first LEGO ship designed to float is released.
- LEGO Systems Inc. USA and LEGO Portugal are established.

The Expert Series featured more realistic details for experienced builders.

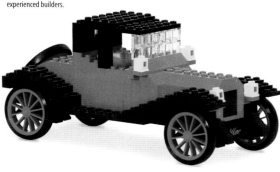

DUPLO figures came with different colours and faces.

## 1975
- The Expert Series of vintage car models is released.
- The LEGO Group now has 2,500 employees.
- LEGO USA moves from Brookfield, Connecticut, to its present location of Enfield, Connecticut.
- A new, smaller LEGO figure is launched with a blank face and non-moving arms and legs.

## 1977
- The LEGO Technic series of mechanical models is launched.

## 1977
- LEGO® DUPLO® sets with door, window and figure elements are launched.

LEGO SCALA featured necklaces and bracelets that girls could build and customise.

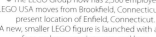

The animal-headed characters of LEGO FABULAND sets had easy-to-construct buildings and vehicles.

## 1979
- Kjeld Kirk Kristiansen, Godtfred Kirk Christiansen's son and Ole Kirk's grandson, is appointed President and Chief Executive Officer of the company.

## 1979
- New products include the FABULAND™ series for young builders and LEGO® SCALA™ jewellery.

# Building the Future

**IN THE 1980s,** the company invested heavily in technology, education and the global community. It sponsored international events like building competitions and awards, developed durable new products for infants and toddlers, created special sets for school programmes and incorporated light and sound into many of its models. New products included buckets full of LEGO® pieces for creative building without instructions, the LEGO Maniac ruled the television screen and the LEGO Pirates set sail ●

## 1980
- The LEGO Educational Products Department is established in Billund.
- The LEGO® DUPLO® rabbit logo is used for the first time.
- 70% of Western European families with children under 14 now have LEGO bricks in their home.

Posable arms and legs

## 1983
- The LEGO DUPLO Baby series is launched, along with new big DUPLO figures with movable arms and legs.
- The company now has 3,700 employees worldwide.

## 1984
- The first international LEGO building competition is held in Billund. Children from 11 countries take part.
- LEGO Brazil and LEGO Korea are established.
- LEGO Castle gains its first factions: the Black Falcons and Crusaders.

## 1985
- The LEGO Prize is founded as an international annual award for exceptional efforts on behalf of children anywhere in the world.
- The company has about 5,000 employees worldwide.

## 1986
- LEGO Technic Computer Control launches in schools.
- The LEGO Technic figure is created.
- The LEGO Group is granted the title "Purveyor to Her Majesty the Queen" on 16 April, the birthday of Queen Margrethe of Denmark.

## 1987
- New products include the motorised LEGO Space Monorail Transport System
- *Brick Kicks*, the official LEGO Club magazine, is mailed to the homes of LEGO Club members across the US.

## 1988
- The first official LEGO World Cup building championships are held in Billund in August. 38 children from 14 countries take part.
- The "Art of LEGO" exhibition tours the United Kingdom.
- LEGO Canada is established.

## 1988
- The "LEGO Maniac" bursts on the scene in a series of TV adverts with a memorable tune, becoming a LEGO mascot for years to come.

## 1981

- The first LEGO World Show takes place in Denmark.

## 1982

- The LEGO Group celebrates its 50th anniversary.
- The LEGO DUPLO Mosaic and LEGO Technic I educational lines launch.
- LEGO South Africa is established.

# Bricks in buckets.

Here they are: The big new LEGO® and DUPLO buckets.
A special offer for more elements. And much space to store a lot more.

## 1986

- Electronic Light & Sound kits are added to LEGO Town and LEGO Space.

## 1987

- The LEGO Club starts in Germany, Austria, Switzerland, France and Norway.
- Buckets are sold containing basic LEGO and LEGO DUPLO elements.
- Launch of the Space sub-themes Blacktron and Futuron.

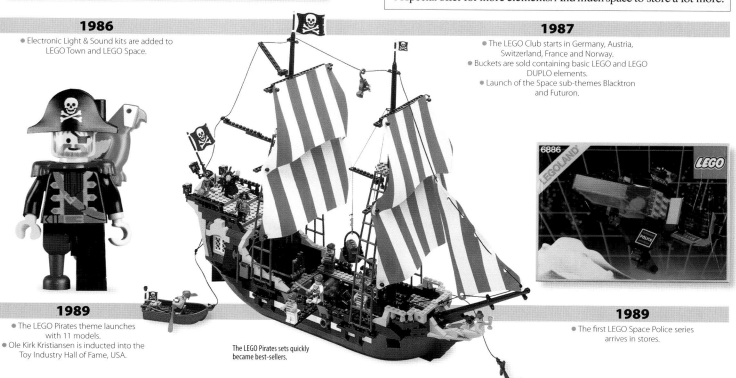

## 1989

- The LEGO Pirates theme launches with 11 models.
- Ole Kirk Kristiansen is inducted into the Toy Industry Hall of Fame, USA.

The LEGO Pirates sets quickly became best-sellers.

## 1989

- The first LEGO Space Police series arrives in stores.

# LEGO® Catalogues

**SINCE THE DEBUT** of the LEGO® System of Play, the company's mission has been to let parents and children know about all the different ways to play with LEGO bricks. For decades, colourful, informative and fun-filled LEGO brand catalogues have displayed the very latest exciting LEGO sets and themes. Here is just a small selection of catalogues, all of which have inspired, or continue to inspire, LEGO fans around the world to new heights of creativity ●

1959

Your guide to the world of LEGO® 1974

1974

Legoland 11

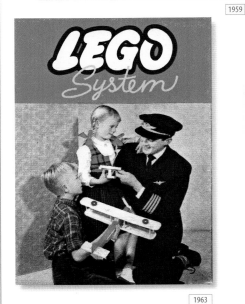

1963

1981

LEGO® & DUPLO Catalogue '84

1984

PLANPACKS

1969

**9-14 years**

### Technical Sets for experienced builders

LEGO Technical Sets are for skilled builders of 9 and over who enjoy the challenge of creating realistic detailed working models. Working pistons, differential gears, steering mechanisms and power transmission are just some of the impressive features to be found in these Technical Sets. Detailed construction diagrams are included in each set and now there's a new Technical Ideas Book to help you design working models of your own.

1981

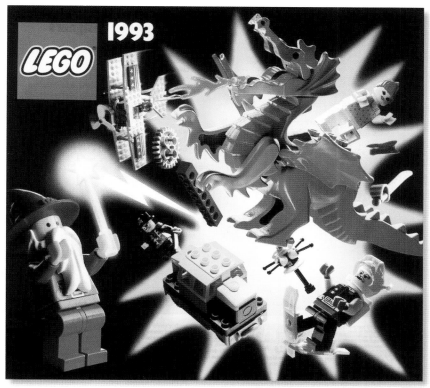

1993

They are building a relationship.

2-6 year

1997

1999

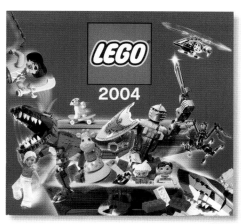

2004

2009

2012 January-June

2012

# Full Speed Ahead!

**THE 1990s** were a time of big risks for a company that had become one of the world's largest toy manufacturers. The decade saw the opening of stores that sold only LEGO® products, a branded clothing shop, the first LEGO video games, the launch of the official LEGO website, the release of a high-tech building system for constructing programmable robots and a leap into licensed themes with the record-smashing debut of LEGO® *Star Wars*™ ●

## 1990

● The LEGO Group is now one of the world's ten largest toy manufacturers and the only one of the ten in Europe.
● LEGOLAND® Billund gets over 1 million visitors in a single year.
● LEGO Malaysia is established.
● The Model Team series and the LEGO® DUPLO® Zoo are launched.

DUPLO PRIMO figures

## 1993

● A LEGO building event takes place in Red Square in Moscow, Russia.
● LEGO Space travels to the Ice Planet 2002.

## 1994

● The United Nations Commission on Human Rights (UNCHR) uses LEGO minifigures as part of an awareness campaign.
● The LEGO® BELVILLE™ line of building sets for girls is released.
● LEGO Mexico is established.
● LEGO products are advertised on Chinese television for the first time.
● The company has 8,880 employees worldwide.
● *Brick Kicks* becomes *LEGO Mania* magazine.

## 1995

● Godtfred Kirk Christiansen passes away.
● Weekly LEGO programs air on TV in Latvia and Lithuania.
● LEGO events and exhibitions take place in Latvia, Peru, Hungary, Switzerland, Denmark, Greenland, the US, Canada, Italy and Ecuador.
● LEGO Aquazone and DUPLO® PRIMO™ are launched.

## 1997

● More than 300,000 children take part in a LEGO building event at Kremlin Palace in Moscow, Russia.
● The LEGO Kids Wear shop opens in Oxford Street, London, UK.

## 1998

● The company adopts the slogan "Just Imagine…"
● Japanese Emperor Akihito and Empress Michiko visit LEGOLAND Billund.
● The LEGO® MINDSTORMS® and Znap lines launch.

## 1998

● The LEGO logo is updated.
● The LEGO Space Insectoids appear.
● The LEGO Adventurers explore Egypt.

## 1991

- The company now has 7,550 employees and 1,000 injection-moulding machines at the five LEGO factories.
- New products include the LEGO Town Harbor sets, Technic flex-system elements, and transformer-controlled 9-volt trains.

## 1991

- The LEGO System Brick Vac helps pick bricks up off the floor.
- The LEGO Town Nautica series starts.

## 1992

- The first LEGO Imagination Centre opens at the Mall of America in Bloomington, Minneapolis, USA.
- The world's largest LEGO Castle is built on Swedish television out of more than 400,000 bricks.
- The second LEGO World Cup Final in Billund features 32 children competing from 11 countries.
- Paradisa and Res-Q sets are released for LEGO Town.

Fort LEGOREDO, the wildest Wild West set of them all!

## 1996

- LEGOLAND® Windsor opens in the UK.
- The official LEGO website, www.LEGO.com, goes online.
- LEGOLAND Billund receives its 25-millionth visitor.

## 1996

- LEGO Western and LEGO Time Cruisers are launched.

## 1997

- The LEGO Island computer game is released.
- A new LEGO Imagination Centre opens in Disney Village, Florida, USA.
- The first LEGO® MINDSTORMS® Learning Centre opens at the Museum of Science and Industry in Chicago, Illinois, USA.

The first year's sets included models from the classic trilogy and the brand-new prequel movie.

## 1999

- LEGOLAND® California opens in Carlsbad, CA, USA.
- Fortune Magazine names the LEGO brick one of the "Products of the Century."
- The LEGO World Shop opens at www.LEGO.com.
- New LEGO themes include Rock Raiders, LEGO® DUPLO® Winnie the Pooh and Friends™ and one of the biggest ever: LEGO® Star Wars™.

# New Worlds to Discover

**MANY EXCITING** new sets were released during the first few years of the millennium, including several licensed characters – from super heroes to talking sponges. The first LEGO® figures based on real people were produced, changing the familiar yellow face of the minifigure forever. The company even created its own new worlds with original science fiction and fantasy themes complete with stories that were told through books, comics and films ●

## 2000
● The British Association of Toy Retailers names the LEGO brick "Toy of the Century."
● The LEGO Sports theme launches with LEGO Soccer/Football.
● LEGO Studios launches, letting budding film-makers build and animate their own LEGO movies.
● Disney's Baby Mickey™ sets are released.

## 2002
● LEGO Studios introduces the first ever Vampire in a frightfully fun new set.
● LEGOLAND® Deutschland opens in Günzburg.
● "Play On" replaces "Just Imagine…" as the company slogan.

## 2002
● LEGO Island Xtreme Stunts sets based on the video game arrive.
● Galidor: Defenders of the Outer Dimension, based on the TV series, features action figures with swappable body parts.
● LEGO Racers teams compete in the Racing Drome, with an accompanying video game.
● *LEGO Mania* magazine becomes *LEGO Magazine*.
● LEGO® DUPLO® becomes LEGO Explore and introduces LEGO® Bob the Builder™ sets.
● LEGO Brand Retail stores open in Germany, England and Russia.

## 2003
● The LEGO minifigure celebrates its 25th birthday.
● LEGO Sports NBA Basketball and Hockey sets join the game.
● LEGO® Dora the Explorer™ sets are released under LEGO Explore.

## 2004
● LEGO EXPLORE is replaced by three building systems for the very young: LEGO DUPLO, BABY and QUATRO.
● The US LEGO Club creates the premium LEGO BrickMaster programme.
● LEGO Factory lets builders create models online and buy the pieces to make them.
● Several traditional LEGO brick colours are retired and new colours are introduced.

## 2005
● LEGO Dino Attack and LEGO Dino 2010 roar to life.
● The LEGO System of Play celebrates its 50th anniversary.
● The LEGOLAND parks are sold to the Merlin Entertainments Group. The LEGO Group owners maintain a shareholding in Merlin Entertainments Group.

## 2005
● The LEGO Vikings set sail.
● The first LEGO® *Star Wars*™ video game is released.
● LEGO *Star Wars*: Revenge of the Brick airs on television.

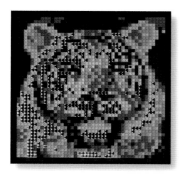

## 2000

- The LEGO KNIGHTS' KINGDOM series launches.
- LEGO Writing office and school supplies are introduced.
- LEGO Mosaic lets you create your face in LEGO bricks.
- Action Wheelers brings racing action into younger hands.
- LEGO Arctic unleashes the first LEGO polar bear.
- The LEGO Adventurers travel to Dino Island.

## 2001

- The BIONICLE® line launches worldwide with a huge publicity campaign.
- The magic of LEGO® Harry Potter™ begins.
- Jack Stone rescues his city from natural disasters in a new "4 Plus" figure scale for younger builders.
- The LEGO Dinosaurs line is hatched.

## 2001

- LEGO® SERIOUS PLAY™ is founded to help businesses learn creative thinking through the use of LEGO bricks and building.
- Life on Mars takes LEGO Space to the Red Planet.

## 2001

- The LEGO Alpha Team battles to save the world from the evil Ogel.
- LEGO Racers starts its engine with a line of crashing mini-cars with alien drivers.

## 2003

- LEGO Town becomes LEGO World City.
- LEGO Discovery NASA sets based on modern space exploration are released. LEGO Minifigure astrobots Biff Starling and Sandy Moondust – or pictures of them, at least – become the first Earthlings to reach the planet Mars aboard the NASA rovers *Spirit* and *Opportunity*.

## 2003

- The CLIKITS™ line of buildable jewellery is released.
- The BIONICLE film *Mask of Light* is released to DVD.
- LEGO Designer and LEGO Gravity Games lines are launched.
- A record-breaking 1.63 million people visit LEGOLAND Billund.
- Little Robots™ toys are released in Europe based on the TV series.
- www.LEGO.com receives about 4 million visitors per month.

## 2004

- The second LEGO KNIGHTS' KINGDOM series is released.
- The LEGO Group partners with Ferrari to create a line of licensed LEGO Racers sets.
- *BIONICLE 2: Legends of Metru Nui* is released on DVD.

## 2005

- LEGO Racers shrinks race cars down into pocket-sized Tiny Turbos.
- LEGO DUPLO introduces Thomas and Friends™ building sets.
- LEGO World City is renamed LEGO City.

## 2006

- The new LEGO® EXO-FORCE™ theme begins, inspired by Japanese giant-robot comics and animation.
- LEGO® MINDSTORMS® NXT is launched.
- LEGO® Batman™ leaps onto the scene.

## 2006

- Remote-controlled LEGO Trains replace the classic electric system.
- LEGO sets based on the Nickelodeon cartoons *SpongeBob SquarePants*™ and *Avatar: The Last Airbender*™ are released.
- LEGO *Star Wars* II: The Original Trilogy video game is released.

# And Beyond!

**THE COMPANY CELEBRATED** its 75th anniversary in 2007, and things only got bigger from there. LEGO® construction returned to outer space, and classic Castle, Pirates and underwater themes made triumphant comebacks as well. Licensed lines were a huge success with blockbuster video games and sets based on some of the biggest properties around, from comic books to hobbits. These years also saw a boom for ninja, the debut and demise of LEGO Universe, and the 30th anniversary of the one and only LEGO minifigure ●

### 2007

- The LEGO Group celebrates its 75th anniversary.
- LEGO Mars Mission brings back LEGO Space sets for the first time since 2001's Life on Mars.
- More classic themes return in the form of new LEGO Castle and LEGO Aqua Raiders product lines.

### 2008

- LEGOLAND Discovery Center Chicago opens in Schaumberg, IL, USA.
- LEGO Stores begin offering a monthly mini-model build event.
- The LEGO Architecture theme introduces special-edition microscale models of famous buildings.

### 2009

- LEGO Games is launched.
- LEGO Power Miners launches.
- The LEGO *Star Wars* theme celebrates its 10th anniversary with special packaging and minifigures.
- The LEGO Indiana Jones 2: The Adventure Continues video game is released.
- LEGO Rock Band puts a minifigure spin on the Rock Band series of music video games.

### 2009

- The LEGO Agents upgrade to Agents 2.0.
- LEGO City branches out into the countryside with LEGO Farm sets.
- LEGO fans use the LEGO Design byME programme to build virtual 3D models and order them online with a custom box and building instructions.
- LEGO Pirates and LEGO Space Police return with all-new sets.

### 2010

- LEGO World Racers takes builders on a frenetic, action-packed race through different environments.
- The long-running BIONICLE line comes to an end with the release of six BIONICLE Stars commemorative sets, each with a piece of extra golden armour to upgrade the Tahu figure.
- Harry Potter sets are produced for the first time since 2007.

### 2011

- Aliens invade Earth with LEGO Alien Conquest sets.
- Hero Recon Team lets builders create their own Hero Factory characters online and order the parts through the post.
- After a decade, LEGO® DUPLO® Winnie the Pooh™ sets return.

### 2012

- The LEGO Friends theme introduces a new line of building sets aimed at girls.
- World-famous heroes and villains take the LEGO world by storm with the debut of the LEGO DC Universe Super Heroes and LEGO Marvel Universe Super Heroes themes.
- The LEGO® *The Lord of the Rings*™ theme is released.

### 2012

- Dinosaurs threaten the modern world once again with LEGO Dino.
- LEGO Ninjago gets an entire season of half-hour television episodes.
- New LEGOLAND Discovery Centers open in Kansas City and Atlanta.

### 2012

- The LEGO Monster Fighters battle classic monster villains to prevent the sun from being forever extinguished.
- LEGO CUUSOO voting leads to the production of a LEGO® Minecraft™ licensed model.
- LEGO DUPLO Disney Princess sets are released

Indy's whip, hat and bag were all-new pieces for 2008.

## 2007
- The LEGO® Star Wars™: The Complete Saga video game lets gamers play through a brick-ified version of all six films.
- The Modular Buildings series of models for advanced builders launches with the Café Corner set.
- Mr Magorium's Big Book, a set containing nine different models, is released to coincide with the film Mr Magorium's Wonder Emporium.
- LEGO Creator sets introduce LEGO Power Functions – electronic modules that add motors, lights and remote-controlled movement to models.

## 2008
- Kjeld Kirk Kristiansen is inducted into the Toy Industry Hall of Fame, USA.
- LEGO Magazine becomes LEGO Club Magazine.
- The first issue of LEGO Club Jr. magazine is sent to younger club members in the US.

## 2008
- The LEGO® Indiana Jones™, LEGO® Speed Racer™ and LEGO Agents themes are launched.
- LEGO Indiana Jones and LEGO® Batman™ videogames are released.

## 2008
- The 50th anniversary of the patent of the stud-and-tube LEGO brick is celebrated with a worldwide building contest.
- The 30th birthday of the LEGO minifigure is commemorated with the "Go Miniman Go!" internet campaign and fan-video showcase.

## 2010
- The LEGO Universe massively multiplayer online game is released.
- The LEGO Minifigures line launches with its first series of 16 characters.
- The LEGO Group and Disney resume their partnership with the release of sets based on the Toy Story films, Cars (in LEGO® DUPLO® form) and Prince of Persia.

## 2011
- LEGO Ninjago puts a whole new spin on martial-arts action.
- The legacy of the LEGO Adventurers lives on with the heroes of the Pharaoh's Quest theme.
- Life of George is released as an iPhone/iPod Touch application that interacts with a LEGO set.
- LEGO® Pirates of the Caribbean™ sets include ships, locations and characters from the blockbuster films.

## 2011
- LEGOLAND® Florida becomes North America's second LEGOLAND theme park.
- A LEGOLAND Discovery Center opens in Texas.
- LEGOLAND California adds a new Star Wars section to its MINILAND display.
- LEGO Star Wars III: The Clone Wars introduces video game missions based on the computer-animated television series.

## 2011
- LEGO City gains a new spaceport with sets developed in conjunction with NASA.
- LEGO sets are launched into space aboard the Space Shuttle Endeavour.
- The LEGO CUUSOO partnership lets fans vote for models to be considered for release as LEGO sets.

## 2013
- The LEGO® Legends of CHIMA™ theme introduces fans to the amazing animal tribes of Chima and their action-packed adventures.
- The LEGO® DUPLO® Planes™ theme takes off.
- The LEGO® Teenage Mutant Ninja Turtles™ theme debuts.

## 2013
- The LEGO Galaxy Squad defends the universe from the evil alien Buggoids and Mosquitoids.
- The LEGO castle theme returns.
- New LEGOLAND Discovery Centers open in Oberhausen, Germany and Westchester, New York.

## 2014
- The LEGO® Movie is released in cinemas worldwide. A theme and series of minifigures accompany the film.
- The LEGO® Mixels™ and the LEGO® Simpsons™ themes are introduced.
- LEGO IDEAS replaces LEGO CUUSOO.

# The LEGO® Brick Patent

**WHEN THE LEGO GROUP** launched the LEGO® System of Play in 1955, it realised that the new LEGO brick had to be as perfect a building toy as possible. Bricks needed to lock together firmly to make stable models, but also come apart easily. CEO Godtfred Kirk Christiansen was determined to perfect the brick's quality and clutch power and fulfill the company's belief that it should be possible to build virtually *anything* with LEGO elements. At 1:58 pm on 28 January 1958, he finally submitted an application in Copenhagen, Denmark, for a patent for the improved LEGO brick and its building system ●

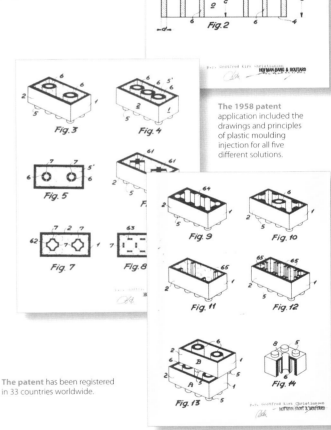

The 1958 patent application included the drawings and principles of plastic moulding injection for all five different solutions.

The patent has been registered in 33 countries worldwide.

### THE STUD-AND-TUBE SOLUTION

The company developed several possible ways to improve the brick's clutch power. The first added three tubes to the underside of the current LEGO brick, creating a perfect three-point connection with the studs on top of the next brick below. Alternative solutions included bricks with two tubes or even crosses inside, with a total of five potential connection methods.

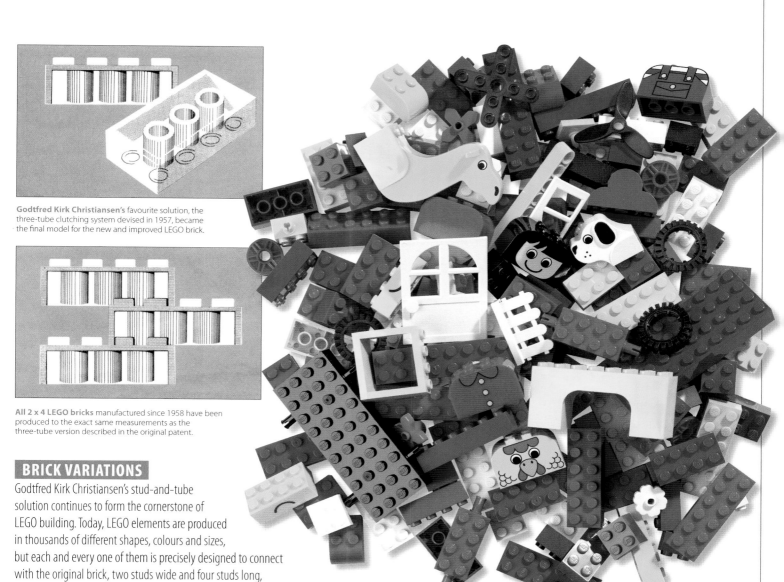

**Godtfred Kirk Christiansen's** favourite solution, the three-tube clutching system devised in 1957, became the final model for the new and improved LEGO brick.

**All 2 x 4 LEGO bricks** manufactured since 1958 have been produced to the exact same measurements as the three-tube version described in the original patent.

## BRICK VARIATIONS

Godtfred Kirk Christiansen's stud-and-tube solution continues to form the cornerstone of LEGO building. Today, LEGO elements are produced in thousands of different shapes, colours and sizes, but each and every one of them is precisely designed to connect with the original brick, two studs wide and four studs long, that was patented on that famous day in 1958.

### UNLIMITED POSSIBILITIES

The patented clutching ability of the LEGO brick gives builders of all ages an almost infinite variety of ways to express their imagination and creativity through construction. Each brick in the system can be connected to every other brick in multiple configurations, and as more bricks are added, the possibilities grow exponentially.

**Two eight-stud** LEGO bricks can be combined in 24 ways.

**Three eight-stud** LEGO bricks can be combined in 1,060 ways.

**Six eight-stud** LEGO bricks can be combined in 915,103,765 ways.

**With eight bricks,** the possibilities are virtually endless.

# The LEGO® Logo

**SINCE ITS CREATION** in 1934, the LEGO® logo has undergone many changes. By 1953, what was affectionately nicknamed the "sausage logo" – rounded, black-outlined white letters and a red background – already resembled today's distinctive brand. By the early 1970s, the logo looked almost as it does today; a slight modification in 1998 brought it up to date ●

**1934**

**1950**

**1946**

**1953**

**1955**

**1955**

**1958**

**1958**

**1936**

**1946**

**1953**

**1953**

**1956**

**1958**

**1958**

**1964**

**1972**

**1998**

# THE LEGO® BRICK

● LEGO® elements are part of a universal system and are all compatible with each other; bricks from 1958 fit bricks made 50 years later ● At 1:58 pm on 28 January 1958, the company received a patent to manufacture LEGO bricks ● Since 1963, LEGO elements have been manufactured from ABS (acrylonitrile butadiene styrene), which is scratch and bite-resistant ● Bricks are made using small-capacity, precision-made moulds ● Inspectors check the bricks for shape and colour; only an average of 18 out of every million fails the test ● In 2013, over 55 billion LEGO elements were produced. That's approximately 105,000 elements a minute ● Six red eight-stud bricks can be combined in 915,103,765 different ways ● There are more than 2,000 different LEGO brick shapes ● The LEGO brick's 50th anniversary was celebrated in 2008 ● 40 billion LEGO bricks stacked together would reach the Moon ●

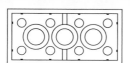

Top view showing studs.    Bottom view showing tubes.

# Making LEGO® Bricks

**THE LEGO®** Kornmarken factory at the company headquarters in Billund, Denmark, opened on 24 June 1987 after 18 months of construction. Today, the giant factory is constantly in motion, operating 24 hours a day and seven days a week. Its workers and state-of-the-art machinery produce about 4 million LEGO elements every hour. Approximately, 31 billion LEGO elements were made there in 2013 alone ●

**The Kornmarken factory** building is big enough for a 20km half-marathon race to be run inside it. It's so big inside that employees often use special scooters and other vehicles to get from place to place quickly.

1

2

3

4

## BRICK BY BRICK BY BRICK...

**1** A LEGO brick begins life as a pile of tiny plastic granules, each about the size of a grain of rice. The granules are shipped to Denmark from Italy, the Netherlands and Germany. There are currently about 50 basic colours, which can be mixed to make additional colours.

**2** The granules are sucked up from large plastic containers into one of the factory's 14 silos.

A silo can hold up to 30 tonnes (33 tons) of granules, but usually contains about 26 tonnes (29 tons). 45 tonnes (50 tons) of granules can be processed every 24 hours.

**3** The granules travel along pipes to one of the 12 moulding halls, which contain a total of 760 moulding machines.

**4** The granules are fed down pipes directly into the moulding machines. A single person,

backed up by maintenance technicians, looks after 65 moulding machines. The machines are computer-controlled and made in Germany and Austria. A warning light on top of the machine turns on to indicate any problems in the moulding process.

**5** Inside the moulding machines, the granules are heated to a temperature of 235ºC (455ºF),

which melts them together into a toothpaste-like mass of gooey plastic. The moulds then apply 25 to 150 tonnes (28 to 165 tons) of pressure (depending on the element being produced) to shape each individual brick to an accuracy of 0.005mm (0.0002in), which is necessary to make sure that every LEGO brick fits together with the rest. In 10–15 seconds,

the bricks harden and cool. Leftover plastic is recycled. Bricks that chance to fall onto the factory floor are also recycled. The new bricks are automatically ejected from the moulds.

**6** The bricks travel along a short conveyor belt, dropping into boxes at the end.

**7** When a box is full of newly made bricks, the moulding machine transmits a signal to

a nearby robot along wires embedded in the floor of the factory.

**8** The robot travels to the machine, collects the box, puts a lid on it, stamps the box with the all-important barcode that enables this particular batch to be identified in future operations and places it on a conveyor belt. This leads to the distribution warehouse.

**9** The box travels along the conveyor belt to the distribution warehouse. The high-level warehouse has space for 424,000 boxes of LEGO® bricks. A logical motion machine, powered by compressed air, finds the boxes according to their barcodes and selects which ones are needed for an order. When certain boxes of bricks are needed to make up a LEGO set, the logical motion machine selects and grabs the correct ones.

**10** The machine places the boxes on a conveyor belt that leads to a truck. The boxes are then driven to the packing, assembling and decoration department.

**11, 12** Assembly machines then attach arms and hands to minifigure bodies, tyres to wheels and so on.

**13** Painting machines add faces to heads and complex patterns to decorated elements.

**14** The finished LEGO pieces are then

transported in trays to the packaging department. Vibrating machines sort the piles of elements into their individual shapes, which are collected in bins. Each bin contains one type of element. Boxes called cassettes move along a conveyor belt beneath the bins. As each cassette arrives beneath a bin, the correct number and type of element drops into it.

**15** The elements are then bagged or stored in clear plastic display trays. Each bag is weighed twice to make sure that it contains the right number and type of elements.

**16** Machines send the bags of elements, along with the set's instruction booklet, down chutes to fall into boxes on a packing line.

**17** LEGO workers check that the bags of elements lie flat so that box lids close tightly.

**18, 19** The boxed LEGO sets are picked up by robotic arms and packed into cardboard boxes for transportation to stores.

# Designing a LEGO® Set

**HOW DO THE LEGO®** set designers come up with all of those wonderful models and minifigures? The first step is finding inspiration. The design team gathers material from many different sources – even from their own experiences. The LEGO City team worked at a fire station for a day to learn more about fire-fighting and fire trucks, and the LEGO Power Miners team took a trip to an underground mine ●

### BRAINSTORMING

Once they have their inspiration, the LEGO design team members get together for a Design Boost session, where they come up with ideas for story, models, characters and any new elements that might be needed. The Design Lead and Marketing Lead refine the models and agree on their price points, making sure that each model is unique, but works as part of the overall series.

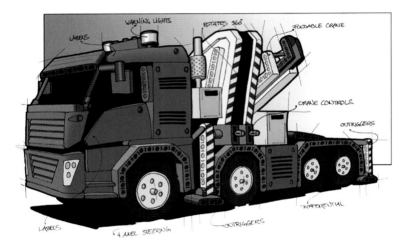

### EARLY CONCEPTS

After the initial brainstorming, some ideas for new sets and minifigures are turned into hand-drawn illustrations or clay character models, while others are built out of LEGO bricks as conceptual "sketch models." If an element isn't available in the right colour, the designers paint it themselves.

### CREATING NEW ELEMENTS

If the set needs a new LEGO element, the model designer works with a part designer or engineer to produce it. Rounded pieces like animals and minifigure hair are hand-sculpted and scanned into a computer for the engineer to finalise, while simple shapes like bricks and wheels are built directly on the computer using 3D software.

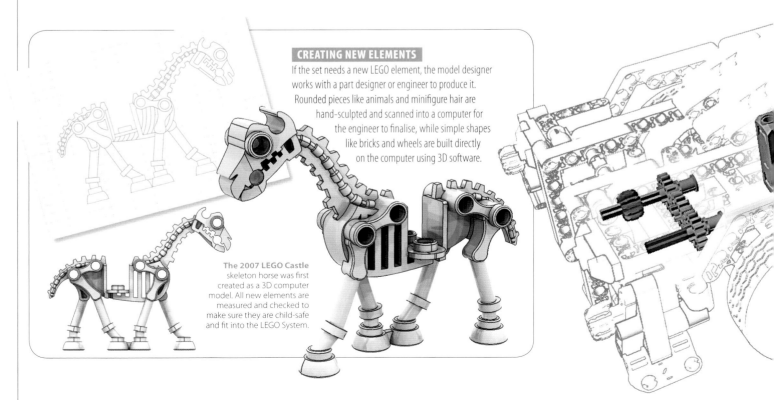

**The 2007 LEGO Castle** skeleton horse was first created as a 3D computer model. All new elements are measured and checked to make sure they are child-safe and fit into the LEGO System.

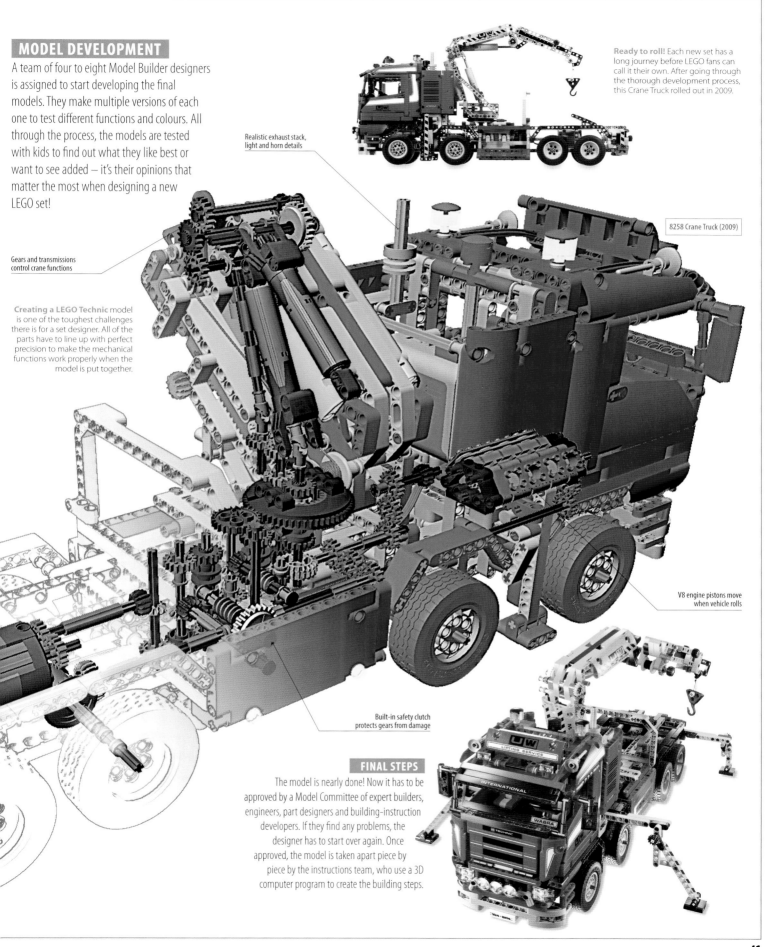

## MODEL DEVELOPMENT

A team of four to eight Model Builder designers is assigned to start developing the final models. They make multiple versions of each one to test different functions and colours. All through the process, the models are tested with kids to find out what they like best or want to see added – it's their opinions that matter the most when designing a new LEGO set!

**Ready to roll!** Each new set has a long journey before LEGO fans can call it their own. After going through the thorough development process, this Crane Truck rolled out in 2009.

Realistic exhaust stack, light and horn details

8258 Crane Truck (2009)

Gears and transmissions control crane functions

**Creating a LEGO Technic** model is one of the toughest challenges there is for a set designer. All of the parts have to line up with perfect precision to make the mechanical functions work properly when the model is put together.

V8 engine pistons move when vehicle rolls

Built-in safety clutch protects gears from damage

### FINAL STEPS

The model is nearly done! Now it has to be approved by a Model Committee of expert builders, engineers, part designers and building-instruction developers. If they find any problems, the designer has to start over again. Once approved, the model is taken apart piece by piece by the instructions team, who use a 3D computer program to create the building steps.

**Inspirational building** leaflet included in LEGO model boxes between 1963 and 1964.

# LEGO® Play Themes

**EVEN THOUGH** all of the sets in the LEGO® System of Play were designed to be compatible within one big creative LEGO universe, there were some types of models that kids wanted more and more of. More trains! More castles! More cities! More spaceships! Answering the call in 1978 were the first three LEGO Play Themes, each full of sets based on a popular subject and populated by the brand-new, fully-posable LEGO minifigures. LEGO Castle had medieval knights, kings and fortresses. LEGO Town had buildings, roads, cars and trucks. LEGO Space had rockets, rovers and lunar bases. No matter what your favourite theme was, now you could collect and construct it to build your own LEGO world ●

# LEGO® Town & City

**SOME THINGS** never go out of style in the big city. While LEGO® Town and LEGO City sub-themes may have come and gone over the years, no brick-built metropolis is complete without these classic civic fixtures: a police department, a fire station, an airport, a hospital and a busy construction crew to ensure the city keeps on growing ●

With a moving piston and bucket, the Fire Station engine's folding, telescoping ladder worked just like the real thing.

Fire truck from 7945 Fire Station (2007)

### FIRE

For more than 50 years, the fearless firefighters of LEGO City have been extinguishing blazes and saving LEGO cats from LEGO trees with the help of extending ladders, wind-up hoses and an ever-growing assortment of fire engines, fire stations and rescue gear!

**Not everyone** rides in the truck. When there's an emergency in LEGO City, the Fire Chief speeds to the scene in his personal car.

### POLICE

When danger calls, the LEGO City Police are always on the scene. These dedicated officers never stop patrolling the streets of LEGO City, protecting its citizens night and day. From their modern police station, they can monitor radio bands, dispatch vehicles to emergencies, scan the crime computer and keep watch on the prison in case of break-outs.

7892 LEGO City Hospital (2006)

**The most common** procedure at this hospital? Emergency minifigure reassembly!

**The operating room** had everything a LEGO doctor could need. Just don't ask about the chainsaw in the corner.

### HOSPITAL

Though it's had fewer releases than the other major sub-themes, the LEGO City Hospital is a vital part of city life. Complete with all the latest innovations in minifigure medical care, it even had a helicopter pad and off-road vehicle for the biggest emergencies in and out of town.

7744 Police Headquarters (2008)

Radio mast

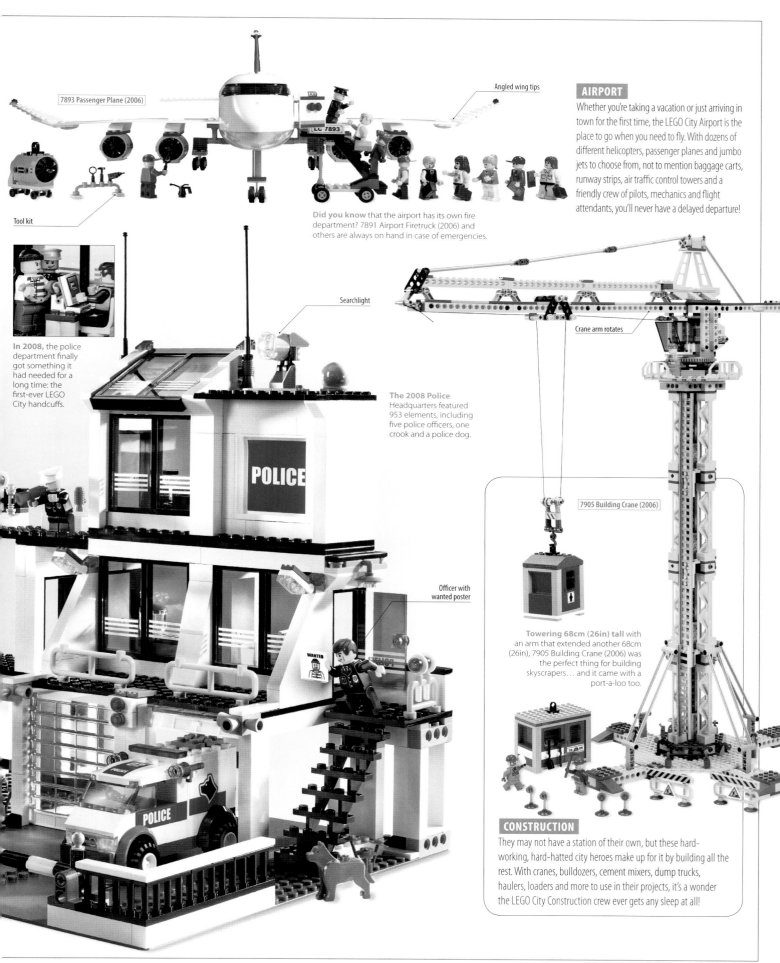

7893 Passenger Plane (2006)

Angled wing tips

Tool kit

## AIRPORT

Whether you're taking a vacation or just arriving in town for the first time, the LEGO City Airport is the place to go when you need to fly. With dozens of different helicopters, passenger planes and jumbo jets to choose from, not to mention baggage carts, runway strips, air traffic control towers and a friendly crew of pilots, mechanics and flight attendants, you'll never have a delayed departure!

**Did you know** that the airport has its own fire department? 7891 Airport Firetruck (2006) and others are always on hand in case of emergencies.

**In 2008,** the police department finally got something it had needed for a long time: the first-ever LEGO City handcuffs.

Searchlight

**The 2008 Police** Headquarters featured 953 elements, including five police officers, one crook and a police dog.

Crane arm rotates

7905 Building Crane (2006)

POLICE

Officer with wanted poster

WANTED

POLICE

**Towering 68cm (26in) tall** with an arm that extended another 68cm (26in), 7905 Building Crane (2006) was the perfect thing for building skyscrapers… and it came with a port-a-loo too.

## CONSTRUCTION

They may not have a station of their own, but these hard-working, hard-hatted city heroes make up for it by building all the rest. With cranes, bulldozers, cement mixers, dump trucks, haulers, loaders and more to use in their projects, it's a wonder the LEGO City Construction crew ever gets any sleep at all!

# Sets to Remember

374 Fire Station (1978)

376 Town House With Garden (1978)

6365 Summer Cottage (1981)

6380 Emergency Treatment Center (1987)

6335 Indy Transport (1996)

600 Police Car (1978)

1572 Super Tow Truck (1986)

6414 Dolphin Point (1995)

1656 Evacuation Team (1991)

6356 Med-Star Rescue Plane (1988)

6336 Launch Response Unit (1995)

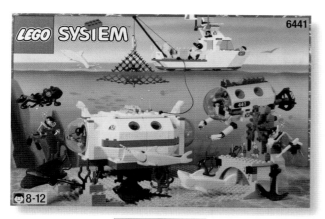

6441 Deep Reef Refuge (1997)

10159 City Airport (2004)

6473 RES-Q Cruiser (1998)

7239 Fire Truck (2004)

6435 Coast Guard HQ (1999)

7634 Tractor (2009)

7734 Cargo Plane (2008)

7034 Surveillance Truck (2003)

7631 Dump Truck (2009)

7279 Police Minifigure Collection (2011)

# LEGO® Train

**ALL ABOARD!**

Train conductor (2003)

**This conductor's** jacket bears the LEGO Train logo.

**IT'S BEEN SPEEDING** down the tracks since 1966. It's driven on blue rails, grey rails, metal rails and plastic rails. It's been powered by hand, clockwork, batteries, electricity and remote control. From old-time steam locomotives to modern bullet trains, here comes that classic among classics: the famous LEGO® Train ●

7740

### INTER-CITY EXPRESS

This German inter-city engine with an electric 12-volt motor and two passenger cars was introduced in 1980, the year when the LEGO Train theme was redesigned with grey tracks and a more realistic model style.

7740 12V Passenger Train (1980)

**Most LEGO train cars** were connected to the engine and each other by articulated magnetic couplers; the earliest trains used a hook-and-eye system.

080 Basic Building Set with Train (1967)

### RIGHT ON TRACK

This 700-piece Universal Building Set model included one of the first LEGO trains. It had to be pushed along by hand, but could be motorised with a 4.5-volt battery box borrowed from another train set.

### RUNNING ON BLUE RAILS

Between 1966 and 1979, LEGO train sets ran on blue rails. The first models were basic push-along trains, but 4.5-volt battery motors quickly followed, and in 1969, the latest LEGO trains were powered by 12-volt electrified tracks. Trains of this period were small and low on detail.

182 4.5v Train Set with Signal (1975)

**Thanks to** the LEGO System of Play, boats, aircraft, buildings and trains from different years combine together.

116 Starter Train Set with Motor (1967)

**Blue LEGO train** tracks were simple rails with white cross-tie bricks to hold them off the ground.

L-386

113 Motorized Train Set (1966)

10020 Santa Fe Super Chief (2002)

## SANTA FE SUPER CHIEF

Originally sold as a numbered limited edition of 10,000, this locomotive was based on the real *Super Chief* luxury passenger train. It could be upgraded with additional cars or a motor.

LEGO Train logo

4513 Grand Central Station (2003)

Track-side pizzeria

## RAIL NETWORK

Along with train engines and cars of all shapes and sizes, LEGO Train sets have included a number of stations, level crossings, cargo cranes, a train wash and an engine shed.

6399 Airport Shuttle (1990)

## 9-VOLT MONORAIL

This LEGO Town monorail was powered by the 9-volt electric current that would become a new standard for LEGO Train rails starting in 1991.

## NIGHT TRAIN

Inspired by classic steam engines, the Emerald Night was a LEGO Train fan's dream come true. It measured 68cm (27in) long, featured piston-action wheels and an opening coal tender and dining car and could be motorised by adding Power Functions parts.

10194 Emerald Night (2009)

**The Emerald Night** took a year and a half to develop with input from top train fans. It included two new sizes of big train wheels and elements in new and rare colours.

**This motorised** train would start and stop automatically when you blew the whistle (lying on rear car).

118 Electronic Train (Forward-Stop) (1968)

7897 Passenger Train (2006)

## REMOTE CONTROL

In 2006, LEGO Trains returned to plastic rails and battery-powered motors, but now they had infrared remote controls that could turn on an engine's lights, change its speed and even toot its horn. 2009 saw the further introduction of Power Functions technology, rechargeable motor batteries and new flexible tracks.

**My Own Train** was hosted by Engineer Max and Conductor Charlie, who also came with the 10133 BNSF GP-38 Locomotive set in 2005.

10205 My Own Train (2002)

## MY OWN TRAIN

From 2001 to 2003, the LEGO My Own Train website let builders create and order their own custom trains from two sizes and five colours of classic steam locomotives as well as several types of rolling stock cars.

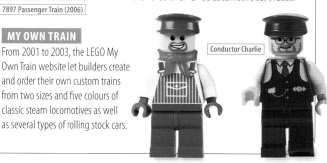

Conductor Charlie

Engineer Max

# Classic Castles

**FROM THE ORIGINAL** yellow castle with its brick-built horses to newer catapult-covered fantasy fortresses, the LEGO® Castle theme has been letting builders create their own medieval kingdoms for more than 30 years. Take a historical tour of some of the most famous castles of the past and present, and then turn the page to discover even more of the world of LEGO Castle ●

375 Castle (1978)

## THE FIRST CASTLE

Here's where it all began! The famous "Yellow Castle" was the very first castle made for the LEGO System of Play. With its tall towers, crank-raised drawbridge and four factions of knights to attack or defend it, it already had many of the classic features of later LEGO castles.

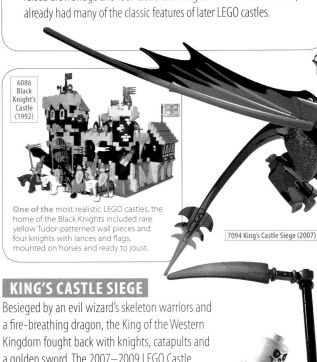

6086 Black Knight's Castle (1992)

**One of the** most realistic LEGO castles, the home of the Black Knights included rare yellow Tudor-patterned wall pieces and four knights with lances and flags, mounted on horses and ready to joust.

You might think that this piece works only as a dragon's wing, but see p. 190 and you might just spot it somewhere else!

7094 King's Castle Siege (2007)

## KING'S CASTLE SIEGE

Besieged by an evil wizard's skeleton warriors and a fire-breathing dragon, the King of the Western Kingdom fought back with knights, catapults and a golden sword. The 2007–2009 LEGO Castle series was praised by fans for its return to classic building styles and castle design, including a working drawbridge and portcullis.

The 2007 Skeleton Warriors were redesigned from the original loose-limbed LEGO Castle skeletons to have scarier skulls and more posable limbs.

8877
Vladek's
Dark
Fortress
(2005)

**Bad guys** need homes too. When the evil Vladek conquered the kingdom of Ankoria, he built his own fortress, complete with launching fireballs and an enchanted mask for the heroes to knock off its central tower.

Watch out if you walk from the treasure room to the prison tower. This bridge is booby-trapped to flip upside-down and send attackers flying!

Catapult flings LEGO bricks at the enemy

Break-away wall for battle damage or secret escapes

6097
Night Lord's
Castle
(1997)

**The lair of** the dreaded Fright Knights and their leader, Basil the Bat Lord, was also home to Willa the Witch and a black dragon. Spooky surprises included a secret rotating wall, a locking dungeon door and a skull that appeared inside a crystal ball.

8781 Castle of
Morcia (2004)

**From the second** LEGO® KNIGHTS' KINGDOM™ series, King Mathias's magical castle had reversible details to let you transform it from good and blue to evil and red when the villainous Vladek took control.

6082 Fire Breathing Fortress (1993)

**Starring Majisto** the wizard and his glow -in-the-dark wand, the Dragon Masters series jumped into the world of fantasy and magic. This set featured a rock-dropping dragon head, a cage for captured dragons and a sneaky spy from the Wolfpack Renegades.

6098
King Leo's Castle
(2000)

**From the first** LEGO KNIGHTS' KINGDOM series, this fairy tale-style castle had modular towers on a raised baseplate. It belonged to the Lion Knights, who defended it with the sword-swinging Princess Storm against Cedric the Bull's warriors.

# Sets to Remember

375 Castle (1978)

383 Knight's Tournament (1979)

6074 Black Falcon's Fortress (1986)

6077 Forestmen's River Fortress (1989)

6034 Black Monarch's Ghost (1990)

6030 Catapult (1984)

6059 Knight's Stronghold (1990)

1584 Knight's Challenge (1988)

6049 Viking Voyager (1987)

6062 Battering Ram (1987)

6048 Majisto's Magical Workshop (1993)

6090 Royal Knight's Castle (1995)

6037 Witch's Windship (1997)

LEGO Blacksmith Shop
Schmiedewerkstatt

3739
AGES/EDADES
10+

Building Toy
Jouet de Construction
Juguete para Construir
Cont. 622 pcs/pzs

Original design by Daniel Siskind

3739 Blacksmith Shop (2002)

8702 Lord Vladek (2006)

8823 Mistlands Tower (2006)

6093 Flying Ninja Fortress (1998)

8780 Citadel of Orlan (2004)

7041 Troll Battle Wheel (2008)

8876 Scorpion Prison Cave (2005)

6096 Bull's Attack (2000)

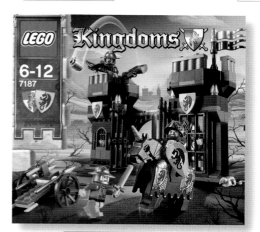
7187 Escape from the Dragon's Prison (2011)

7094 King's Castle Siege (2007)

7949 Prison Carriage Rescue (2010)

53

# Classic LEGO® Space Sets

**THE EARLIEST** LEGO® Space sets in 1978 let kids build a future that seemed just around the corner. The theme became more sci-fi in 1984 with Blacktron and Futuron, the first of many Space sub-series with their own unique vehicle designs, colours, astronauts and model functions. With new series released almost every year through 2001, these sets are the classic era of LEGO Space and beyond ●

**The sleek black spaceships** of Blacktron made it one of the most popular LEGO Space sub-themes. It later provided bad guys for the 1989 Space Police, and was revisited with a second series in 1991.

6954 Renegade (1987)

6990 Monorail Transport System (1987)

### FAST FORWARD
Futuron carried on in the spirit and colour scheme of the original Space sets. Its battery-powered, 9-volt monorail transported blue and yellow astronauts around their home base on a distant moon or planet.

### TO THE STARS
The Unitron theme saw only four sets released in 1994 and 1995, but even this short-lived series had a distinct style. With their translucent blue windows and yellow-green weapons, the high-tech Star Hawk II spaceship, crater cruiser, monorail transport base and Zenon space station were unified by cockpit pods that could be detached and exchanged between vehicles.

1789 Star Hawk II (1995)

Communications dish

Rear laboratory section

### OUT OF THIS WORLD
The earliest LEGO Space sets were a mix of simple science-fiction spaceships, lunar bases, rockets and rovers that weren't too far removed from the real space technology of the 1970s and 1980s, like the Uranium Search Vehicle with its 16 wheels.

6928 Uranium Search Vehicle (1984)

All-terrain wheels

### HEY, MISTER SPACEMAN!
With space suits, helmets and air tanks in white, red, yellow, blue and black, the colorful astronauts of the original LEGO Space series explored the universe in peace and harmony, with no names or stories beyond what builders imagined themselves.

## MINIFIGURE ASTRONAUTS

From M:Tron to Exploriens, U.F.O. and RoboForce, each LEGO Space series had its own astronauts. One rare pair was Biff Starling and Sandy Moondust, "astrobots" produced as a tie-in with NASA's 2003 Mars Exploration Rover mission.

**Space Police II
(1992)**

**Insectoids
(1998)**

**Biff Starling
(2002)**

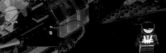
6986 Mission
Commander
(1989)

Rocket booster

## SPACE POLICE

Piloting blue and black vehicles with clear red windows and interchangeable prison cells, the Space Police arrived in 1989 to battle the villains of Blacktron. They returned with a second series in 1992, and again in 2009 after LEGO Space was relaunched.

Classic Space logo

497 Galaxy Explorer (1979)

LL 928

## EXPLORING A GALAXY

The classic of classic LEGO spaceships and a favourite for Space fans, the Galaxy Explorer was built in the traditional blue and grey colour scheme with yellow windows and details. It included a decorated base plate with a communications tower and launch pad.

7314 Recon-Mech RP (2001)

## RED PLANET ADVENTURE

Life on Mars brought things closer to home with the story of a crashed shuttle team and a planet of mech-driving Martians for them to battle or befriend. Apart from a licenced Discovery Channel theme in 2003, it was the last LEGO Space series for six years.

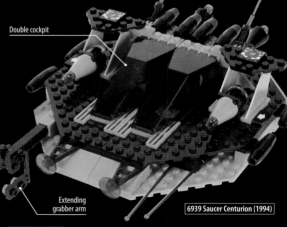

Double cockpit

Extending
grabber arm

6939 Saucer Centurion (1994)

## SPY GUYS

In 1994, Spyrius joined the bad guys of Blacktron as the latest villains to menace the LEGO Space universe. Until 1996, these data-stealing agents used giant and minifigure-sized robots to do their dirty work all over the galaxy. The Saucer Centurion, the Spyrius flagship, could split down the middle to deploy an android-driven space buggy.

## DEEP FREEZE

In 1993, LEGO builders went on an interstellar journey to the distant future of 2002. Ice Planet 2002 took place on the frozen world of Krysto, where clear neon orange parts reigned supreme, jetpacks gave way to skis and lasers were replaced by ice-cutting chainsaws.

Magnetic rocket crane

6898 Ice-Sat V (1993)

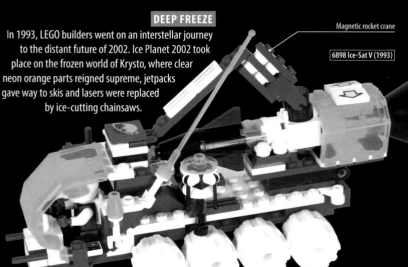

# Sets to Remember

493 Space Command Center (1978)

305 2 Crater Plates (1979)

6954 Renegade (1987)

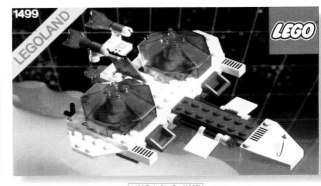

1499 Twin Starfire (1987)

454 Landing Plates (1979)

483 Alpha-1 Rocket Base (1979)

6781 SP-Striker (1989)

6930 Space Supply Station (1983)

6989 Mega Core Magnetizer (1990)

6877 Vector Detector (1990)

6887 Allied Avenger (1991)

6991 Monorail Transport Base (1994)

7315 Solar Explorer (2001)

7699 MT-101 Armoured Drilling Unit (2007)

6939 Sonar Security (1993)

6982 Explorien Starship (1996)

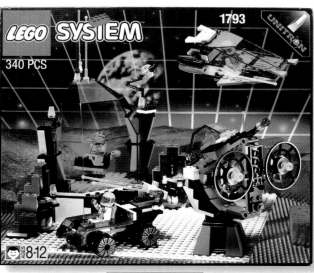

1793 Space Station Zenon (1995)

7697 MT-51 Claw-Tank Ambush (2007)

7647 MX-41 Switch Fighter (2008)

5972 Space Truck Getaway (2009)

6975 Alien Avenger (1997)

6907 Sonic Stinger (1998)

8399 K-9 Bot (2009)

7052 UFO Abduction (2011)

# On The High Seas

**SHIPS AHOY!** A pirate captain has to have a ship, and the LEGO® Pirates theme was filled from the start with gallant galleons, cutlass-laden clippers and ramshackle rafts. Through more than 20 years of ocean-going excitement and fun, these stalwart sea vessels have helped their crews do what they do best: loot, fight and have a swashbucklingly good time on the high seas.

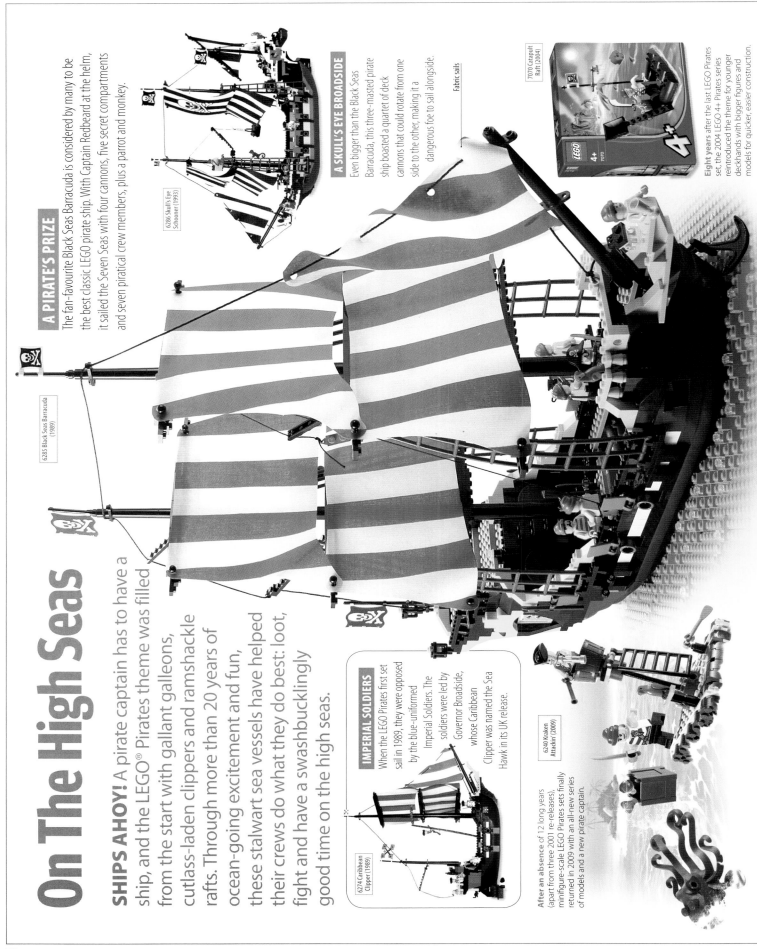

## A PIRATE'S PRIZE

The fan-favourite Black Seas Barracuda is considered by many to be the best classic LEGO pirate ship. With Captain Redbeard at the helm, it sailed the Seven Seas with four cannons, five secret compartments and seven piratical crew members, plus a parrot and monkey.

6286 Skull's Eye Schooner (1993)

## A SKULL'S EYE BROADSIDE

Even bigger than the Black Seas Barracuda, this three-masted pirate ship boasted a quartet of deck cannons that could rotate from one side to the other, making it a dangerous foe to sail alongside.

Fabric sails

7070 Catapult Raft (2004)

**Eight years** after the last LEGO Pirates set, the 2004 LEGO 4+ Pirates series reintroduced the theme for younger deckhands with bigger figures and models for quicker, easier construction.

6285 Black Seas Barracuda (1989)

## IMPERIAL SOLDIERS

When the LEGO Pirates first set sail in 1989, they were opposed by the blue-uniformed Imperial Soldiers. The soldiers were led by Governor Broadside, whose Caribbean Clipper was named the Sea Hawk in its UK release.

6274 Caribbean Clipper (1989)

**After an absence** of 12 long years (apart from three 2001 re-releases), minifigure-scale LEGO Pirates sets finally returned in 2009 with an all-new series of models and a new pirate captain.

6240 Kraken Attackin (2009)

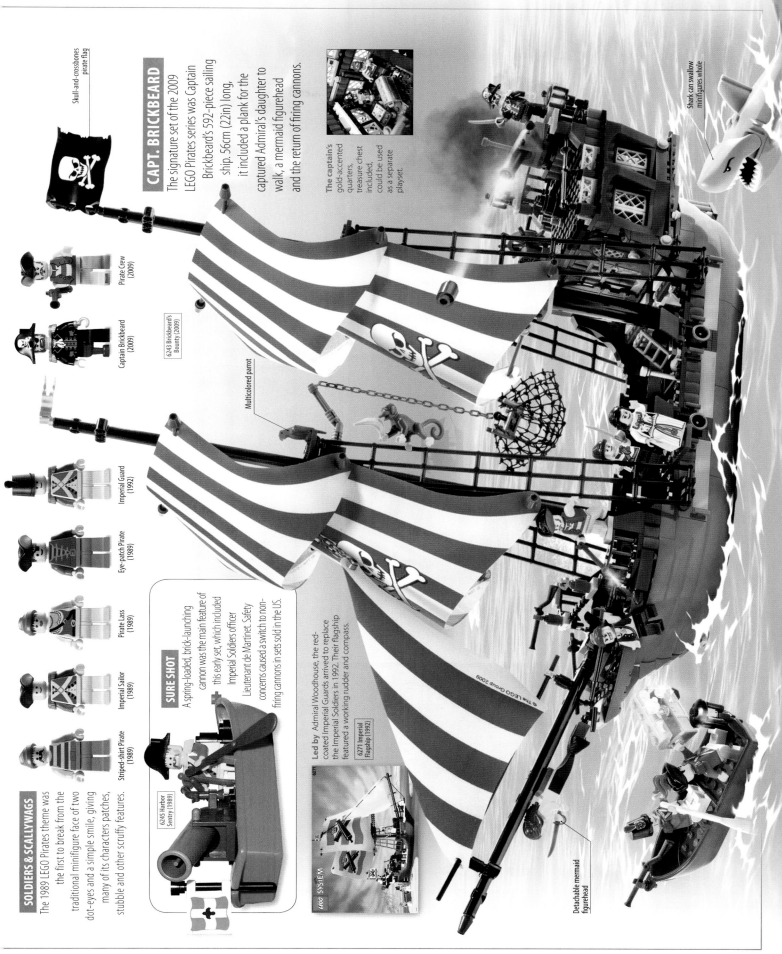

Skull-and-crossbones pirate flag

## CAPT. BRICKBEARD

The signature set of the 2009 LEGO Pirates series was Captain Brickbeard's 592-piece sailing ship. 56cm (22in) long, it included a plank for the captured Admiral's daughter to walk, a mermaid figurehead and the return of firing cannons.

**The captain's** gold-accented quarters, treasure chest included, could be used as a separate playset.

Shark can swallow minifigures whole

Pirate Crew (2009)

Captain Brickbeard (2009)

6243 Brickbeard's Bounty (2009)

Multicolored parrot

Imperial Guard (1992)

Eye-patch Pirate (1989)

Pirate Lass (1989)

Imperial Sailor (1989)

### SURE SHOT

A spring-loaded, brick-launching cannon was the main feature of this early set, which included Imperial Soldiers officer Lieutenant de Martinet. Safety concerns caused a switch to non-firing cannons in sets sold in the US.

Striped-shirt Pirate (1989)

**Led by** Admiral Woodhouse, the red-coated Imperial Guards arrived to replace the Imperial Soldiers in 1992. Their flagship featured a working rudder and compass.

6271 Imperial Flagship (1992)

6245 Harbor Sentry (1989)

## SOLDIERS & SCALLYWAGS

The 1989 LEGO Pirates theme was the first to break from the traditional minifigure face of two dot-eyes and a simple smile, giving many of its characters patches, stubble and other scruffy features.

© The LEGO Group 2009

Detachable mermaid figurehead

# Sets to Remember

6235 Buried Treasure (1989)

1696 Pirate Lookout (1992)

6268 Renegade Runner (1993)

6285 Black Seas Barracuda (1989)

6256 Islander Catamaran (1994)

6262 King Kahuka's Throne (1994)

6236 King Kahuka (1994)

6273 Rock Island Refuge (1991)

6267 Lagoon Lock-up (1991)

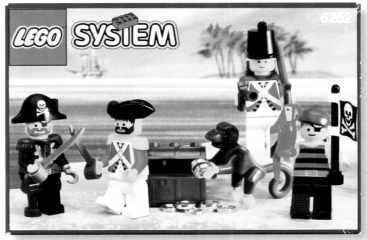
6252 Sea Mates (1993)

6237 Pirates' Plunder (1993)

6279 Skull Island (1995)

6280 Armada Flagship (1996)

6290 Pirate Battle Ship / Red Beard Runner (2001)

8397 Pirate Survival (2009)

1747 Pirates Treasure Suprise (1996)

6296 Shipwreck Island (1996)

6253 Shipwreck Hideout (2009)

6248 Volcano Island (1996)

6232 Skeleton Crew (1996)

8396 Soldier's Arsenal (2009)

6204 Buccaneers (1997)

6249 Pirates Ambush (1997)

7072 Captain Kragg's Pirate Boat (2004)

7071 Treasure Island (2004)

7074 Skull Island (2004)

6241 Loot Island (2009)

# Worlds of Adventure

**FROM THE ROOTIN',** tootin' cowboys of the Wild West to the dangerous world of 2010, from the time-cruising travels of the eccentric Dr Cyber to battles with dinosaurs in the modern-day jungle… when you're building a LEGO® adventure, your imagination can take you anywhere you want to go, or even anywhen – past, present or future ●

6497 Twisted Time Train (1997)

## TIME TRAVEL

In 1996, Dr Cyber, his sidekick Tim and their monkey friend were the LEGO Time Cruisers, bold adventurers who travelled across the centuries in wacky hat-powered contraptions with parts that moved and spun when their wheels turned. 1997 introduced their rivals, Tony Twister and Professor Millennium, also known as the artefact-stealing Time Twisters.

6755 Sheriff's Lock-Up (1996)

## WILD WESTERN

From 1996 to 1997, the LEGO Western theme took builders back to the American frontier of the 1800s and the age of round-ups, showdowns and cattle rustling. With models full of cowboy minifigures, locations and accessories but no official story to set the scene, kids were free to make up their own tall tales and adventures set in the exciting days of the Wild West.

The infamous outlaw Flatfoot Thompson

The brave sheriff and his faithful steed

Card shark Dewey Cheatum

Z-1 Kinetic Launcher

7476 Iron Predator vs. T-Rex (2005)

## LEGO DINO ATTACK

In the near future, mutated monsters from the prehistoric past suddenly appeared and started laying waste to cities all across the globe. Enter the LEGO Dino Attack team: a rag-tag band of scientists, adventurers and soldiers whose mission was to fight back against the rogue reptiles and end their threat once and for all.

## LEGO DINO 2010

In the year 2010, science finally brought extinct dinosaurs back to life. When they broke loose and escaped into the jungle, it was up to a team of fearless dino hunters to track down and recapture the gigantic creatures before they could cause any harm to the outside world.

Light-up eyes and mouth

7297 Dino Track Transport (2005)

**In an unusual** split launch, these 2005 themes offered two different spins on the same basic models. Some countries received the conflict-heavy Dino Attack, with vehicles covered in sci-fi weaponry and firing projectiles, while others had the more peaceful Dino 2010 with its nets, cages and capture gear.

Rotating treads

**Big enough** to carry the tyrant-lizard king himself, this transport chopper included a rolling scout vehicle and a harness designed to lift the largest dino in the line.

5886 T-Rex Hunter (2012)

# LEGO DINO

Two years after 2010 (but seven years after LEGO Dino 2010), dinosaurs once again materialised in the jungle and threatened the nearby city. Another group of daring dino hunters was sent to subdue, capture and study them, armed with powerful tranquilliser weapons and a fleet of heavily armoured all-terrain vehicles.

**Commanded by** Josh Thunder, descendant of Johnny Thunder, the LEGO Dino team's base was built to contain even the toughest T-Rex. The Dino Defense HQ included opening gates, a crane with capture net, a communications centre and lab, two vehicles and three ferocious dinosaurs.

5887 Dino Defense HQ (2012)

## JUNGLE CHASE

Sometimes it takes more than tranq rifles to catch a dinosaur. This off-roader's crew had to lure a ravenous Raptor in close with the most low-tech trap of all: a roasted turkey leg. Then they just needed to snare it with the lasso and somehow get it back to base.

5884 Raptor Chase (2012)

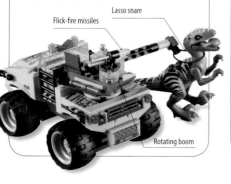

Lasso snare

Flick-fire missiles

Rotating boom

5885 Triceratops Trapper (2012)

## THREE-HORNED TROUBLE

The spikes on the bumper of this heavy-duty truck were no match for the horns of an angry Triceratops. That's why it carried a set of flick-fire tranquilliser missiles in front and a reinforced cage in back. Dino team member "Tracer" Tops was just the minifigure for the job.

**Where did** the dinosaurs come from, and why were they here? The answer was revealed in the pages of *LEGO® Club Magazine*: it was all part of a plot by Commander Hypaxxus-8 of the Alien Conquest theme!

5883 Tower Takedown (2012)

Pteranodon bait stick

Tranq refilling station

Jet boat

# LEGO® *Star Wars*™

**THE LEGO GROUP'S** first licensed property in more than 40 years, LEGO® *Star Wars*™ launched in 1999. With constructible classic vehicles and the whole cast of famous heroes, villains, aliens and droids rendered in minifigure style for the first time ever, the theme was an immediate success with builders of all ages – and it's still proving very popular ●

**7961 Darth Maul's Sith Infiltrator**™ (2011) was the third minifigure-scale version of the ship. It introduced a soft-plastic cap to give Darth Maul his fierce Zabrak horns.

## STAR WARS: EPISODE I *THE PHANTOM MENACE*

### RACE FOR FREEDOM

One of the first sets released from the *Star Wars* prequel trilogy, Mos Espa Podrace let builders pit young Anakin Skywalker and his custom Podracer against rivals Sebulba and Gasgano in a race for his freedom in the perilous Boonta Eve Classic Podrace. With lots of unusual elements and colours, it remains a popular set among LEGO fans. Just like in the movie, Sebulba's orange Podracer was equipped with sneaky gadgets to sabotage his opponents' vehicles.

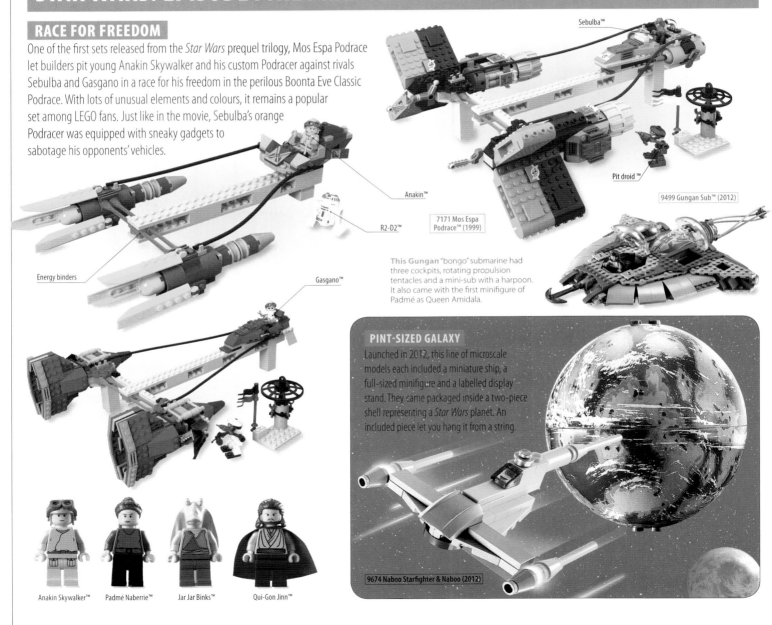

Sebulba™

Anakin™

R2-D2™

Energy binders

Gasgano™

Pit droid™

**7171 Mos Espa Podrace**™ (1999)

**9499 Gungan Sub**™ (2012)

**This Gungan** "bongo" submarine had three cockpits, rotating propulsion tentacles and a mini-sub with a harpoon. It also came with the first minifigure of Padmé as Queen Amidala.

### PINT-SIZED GALAXY

Launched in 2012, this line of microscale models each included a miniature ship, a full-sized minifigure and a labelled display stand. They came packaged inside a two-piece shell representing a *Star Wars* planet. An included piece let you hang it from a string.

**9674 Naboo Starfighter & Naboo** (2012)

Anakin Skywalker™    Padmé Naberrie™    Jar Jar Binks™    Qui-Gon Jinn™

# STAR WARS: EPISODE II *ATTACK OF THE CLONES*

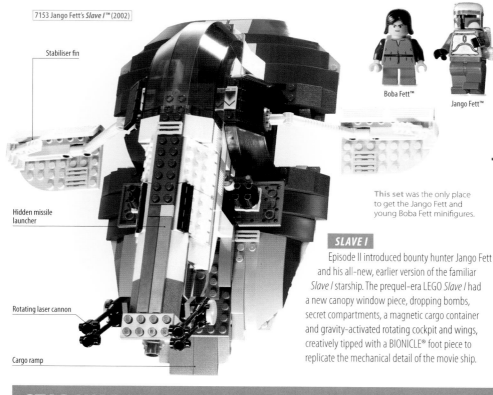

7153 Jango Fett's *Slave I*™ (2002)

Stabiliser fin

Hidden missile launcher

Rotating laser cannon

Cargo ramp

Boba Fett™

Jango Fett™

7163 Republic Gunship™ (2002)

**This set** was the only place to get the Jango Fett and young Boba Fett minifigures.

Super battle droids and destroyer droid

### SLAVE I

Episode II introduced bounty hunter Jango Fett and his all-new, earlier version of the familiar *Slave I* starship. The prequel-era LEGO *Slave I* had a new canopy window piece, dropping bombs, secret compartments, a magnetic cargo container and gravity-activated rotating cockpit and wings, creatively tipped with a BIONICLE® foot piece to replicate the mechanical detail of the movie ship.

### REPUBLIC GUNSHIP

Straight from the final battle on the planet Geonosis, the LEGO Republic Gunship had a 38cm (15in) wingspan, movable side laser turrets, a detachable top section, a magnetic tool-box, opening troop bay doors and hidden compartments. Popular for its many features and a high count of droid and clone trooper minifigures, it also included a mysterious unnamed Jedi Knight to help battle the Separatists. A new, even bigger version of the Republic Gunship was made in 2008 for *The Clone Wars* line.

# STAR WARS: EPISODE III *REVENGE OF THE SITH*

### SPACE BATTLE

The Jedi Knight who would soon become Darth Vader blasted off one last time as a good guy aboard Anakin Skywalker's new Eta-2 interceptor, closely pursued by a Separatist vulture droid that could convert from flight to walking mode. With both hero and villain vehicles included, this set let builders reenact the blazing battle in the skies above Coruscant from the opening scenes of Episode III.

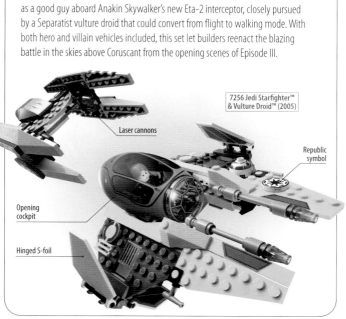

7256 Jedi Starfighter™ & Vulture Droid™ (2005)

Laser cannons

Republic symbol

Opening cockpit

Hinged S-foil

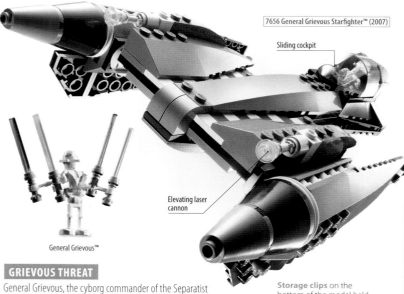

7656 General Grievous Starfighter™ (2007)

Sliding cockpit

Elevating laser cannon

General Grievous™

### GRIEVOUS THREAT

General Grievous, the cyborg commander of the Separatist droid army, piloted this modified Belbullab-22 starfighter during the Clone Wars, but it was Obi-Wan Kenobi who flew away with it after their final battle on Utapau. The model had a slide-open cockpit, flip-up laser cannons and a tail fin that folded down for landing. A new version was released for *The Clone Wars* in 2010.

**Storage clips** on the bottom of the model held the four-armed general's four stolen Jedi lightsabers.

**10179 Ultimate Collector Series
*Millennium Falcon*™ (2008)**

Exhaust vent

Laser cannon

Main sensor

Docking ring

Cockpit

Maintenance access bay

Cargo bay

Forward floodlight

## THE *MILLENNIUM FALCON*

This is it: the biggest LEGO® set ever made! Measuring a whopping 84cm (33in) long, 56cm (22 in) wide and 20.3cm (8in) tall, the Ultimate Collector Series *Millennium Falcon* was built out of 5,195 pieces using the detailed steps in its 311-page, spiral-bound instructions manual. With incredible film-accurate details and moving parts, it quickly became the centrepiece of many a *Star Wars* fan's collection... provided they could find a surface large enough to display it!

**Features included** rotating top and bottom laser turrets, a moving sensor dish, an extending boarding ramp, five minifigures and a display card with technical information about the ship.

**9492 TIE Fighter**™ (2012) included detailed wing panels, flick-firing missiles, an exclusive droid and a new helmet for its Death Star Trooper.

Chewbacca™

Han Solo™

Luke Skywalker™

Princess Leia™

Obi-Wan Kenobi™

## TATOOINE

You'll never build a more wretched hive of scum and villainy. 2004's Mos Eisley Cantina set provided lots of LEGO firsts: the first-ever Dewback riding lizard, the first-ever sandtrooper and the first-ever Greedo minifigure. The desert planet grew with 2012's Droid Escape set, which updated a model from 11 years earlier with new versions of the escape pod, fugitive droids R2-D2 and C-3PO and a pair of Sandtroopers with a swoop bike.

Greedo™

**4501 Mos Eisley
Cantina™ (2004)**

X-34 Landspeeder™

Riding staff

Sandtrooper™

Dewback™

Removable pod cover

Passenger compartment

**9490 Droid™
Escape (2012)**

Maneuvering jet

C-3PO™ with new printing

R2-D2™

Tractor beam targeting array

Command bridge

## STAR DESTROYER

Blasting out of the opening scene of the original *Star Wars* movie, the Ultimate Collector Series Imperial Star Destroyer model stretched nearly 98cm (38½in) long and was made from more than 3,100 pieces. Built more for display than play, it took even advanced builders many hours to assemble the gigantic starship, parts of which were held together with magnets. This model pioneered the use of tiny LEGO elements known as "greebles" to create intricate detail.

Rebel Blockade Runner

Quad laser

Turbolaser turret

**10030 Ultimate Collector Series Imperial Star Destroyer™ (2006)**

**The MINI collection** brought a whole new scale to LEGO *Star Wars*. The first series, including 4484 MINI X-wing vs TIE Advanced (2003), came with pieces to make two pocket-sized models, plus part of a bonus TIE Bomber that could be fully assembled when you collected all 4 sets.

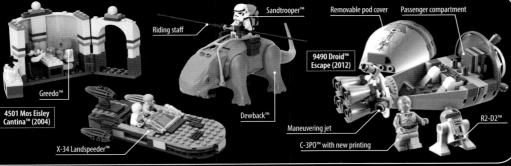

# STAR WARS: EPISODE V *THE EMPIRE STRIKES BACK*

Redesigned Boba Fett

Rotating wing

**8097 Slave I™ (2010)**

**Celebrating the** 30th anniversary of Episode V, this 2010 set featured Boba Fett's version of his ship. It had a carbonite block that could hold Han Solo.

Engine

**In 2006**, this X-wing was re-released without the Episode V elements, but with the first-ever Wedge Antilles™ minifigure and pieces to customise its wing stripes.

S-foil wing

Laser cannon

Storage compartment

**4502 X-wing Fighter™ (2003)**

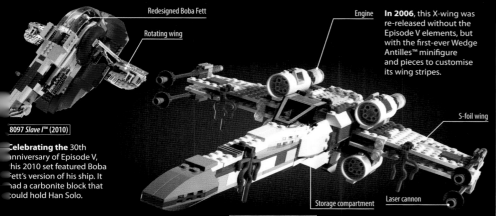

## X-WING FIGHTER

A LEGO X-wing fighter set was released with the first wave of *Star Wars* sets in 1999, but the new 2003 version was a major improvement. It was bigger, had better colors, and was more accurate to the films, plus it came with detachable swamp muck and Yoda's Dagobah hut. The wings were even geared to open and close when you turned a piece on the back of the model!

Yoda™

Luke Skywalker™

**Yoda's hut** opened up to reveal his bed, stew pot, and a secret compartment for his lightsaber.

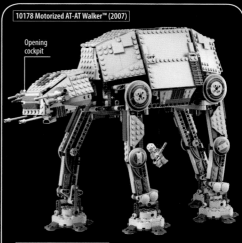

**10178 Motorized AT-AT Walker™ (2007)**

Opening cockpit

## IMPERIAL WALKER

The winner of a 2006 fan vote to decide the next exclusive LEGO *Star Wars* set, the second minifigure-scale AT-AT (All Terrain Armoured Transport) included a LEGO Power Functions motor and battery box. The flip of a switch enabled it to walk forwards or back and move its head. Clever builders added an infrared receiver to make their walkers remote-controlled.

# STAR WARS: EPISODE VI *RETURN OF THE JEDI*

**10143 Death Star II™ (2005)**

## THE SECOND DEATH STAR

An Ultimate Collector Series model designed for assembly by advanced builders 16 and up, the *Death Star II* was made from 3,449 pieces and measured 48cm (19in) across and 63.5cm (25in) high on its display stand. It included translucent pieces to create a firing superlaser beam and a tiny Star Destroyer built to scale with the giant battle station.

## RETURN TO TATOOINE

The LEGO version of Jabba's sail barge was packed with fun play features. You could move the blaster cannon and sails, use the mini-catapult to launch Boba Fett into the air, extend the skiff's gangplank to feed pesky Rebels to the hungry Sarlacc and open the sides to reveal Jabba the Hutt himself, complete with throne room, prison and even a well-stocked kitchen.

**Jabba's 2012** palace included (among others) majordomo Bib Fortuna, dancing girl Oola, monkey-lizard Salacious Crumb, and an all-new Jabba on his throne above the Rancor pit.

**9516 Jabba's Palace™ (2012)**

Forward sail

Jabba the Hutt™

**The Sail Barge** came with eight characters, including Lando Calrissian™ in skiff guard disguise, Princess Leia as Jabba's prisoner, Jedi Luke Skywalker, Han Solo, a Gamorrean guard and R2-D2™ with a drink tray.

Lando™ in disguise

Desert Skiff

Drive thrust system

**6210 Jabba's Sail Barge™ (2006)**

Sarlacc™

# Especially for Girls

**OF COURSE,** there's no rule that says that LEGO® construction is just for boys, and there are plenty of girls who play with exactly the same sets as the other half of the population. But some do prefer construction with a pinker tone, and so we present a sampling of LEGO sets specifically designed for girls ●

5808 The Enchanted Palace (1999)

Glittery, translucent tower

## LEGO® BELVILLE™

Starting in 1994, LEGO BELVILLE introduced a new scale of bigger, multi-jointed figures. With sets that combine traditional LEGO bricks with decorative pink and purple pieces, shiny glitter and lots of horses to ride, the theme included both models of everyday life and scenes from fairy tales and fantasy. A 2005 series featured sets based on classic Hans Christian Andersen stories such as "The Little Mermaid", The Snow Queen", "The Princess and the Pea" and "Thumbelina."

5585 LEGO® Pink Brick Box (2008)

### THINKING PINK

A favourite among grandmothers at holiday time, this sturdy storage box came with fences, windows, doors, flowers and lots of pink bricks mixed in with its 216 pieces for hours of building with a colourful twist.

6411 Sand Dollar Café (1992)

### PARADISA

A sub-theme of LEGO Town that ran from 1992 to 1997, the seaside adventures of Paradisa took place at a tranquil tropical resort. In pastel-coloured sets, Paradisa minifigures enjoyed sailing, windsurfing, beach-side barbecues and playing with friendly dolphins. The colour scheme and settings made Paradisa a very popular theme among girls.

6414 Dolphin Point (1995)

**7538 Totally CLIKITS Fashion Bag and Accessories (2005)**

This set included jewellery, school supplies and a fashion bag to carry them.

## CLIKITS™

A line of buildable, customisable jewelry and accessories, the CLIKITS™ theme featured sets with such fashionable items as photo frames, bracelets and purses, each with connection points to let girls decorate and redesign them with a collection of hearts, stars, seashells and other shapes.

Our website let girls decorate virtual rooms and build digital bracelets to send to their friends!

**4307 Finger Rings (1980)**

## LEGO® SCALA™

CLIKITS wasn't the only line of buildable LEGO jewellery. In 1979, the first LEGO® SCALA™ series let girls use decorated tiles to create their own unique rings, necklaces, bracelets and even a hand mirror. The theme was retired the following year, but it wouldn't be the last time the SCALA name appeared...

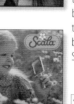

**4336 Mirror (1980)**

Each of the CLIKITS girls had her own colour-coordinated pieces and unique decorations.

**3149 Happy Home (2000)**

## HOUSE AND GARDEN

Unused since 1980, LEGO SCALA was brought back in 1997 as the name of a new dollhouse-style theme. Its characters, including Caroline, Christian, Marie and Baby Thomas, were larger and more traditional fashion dolls than the stylised inhabitants of LEGO BELVILLE. Sets included fabric clothing packs and constructable scenes of gardens, homes and neighbourhood shops.

Foam foliage

**4828 Princess Royal Stables (2007)**

## FAIRY-TALE FUN

With a princess, a prince and three ponies with brushable hair, this LEGO® DUPLO® set was full of fun to spark the imagination of preschool girls.

# LEGO® Friends

**LAUNCHED IN 2012,** the LEGO® Friends theme was designed to provide a fun play experience for girls who couldn't find a perfect match for their building interests in the rest of the LEGO assortment. Its new "mini-doll figures" are slightly taller than minifigures, but they can hold the same objects, connect to the same bricks and even swap hairstyles ●

3061 City Park Café (2012)

## OUT AT THE CAFÉ

The theme centres on the daily lives of five friends who live in the fictional Heartlake City. Its sets feature classic LEGO building, with lots of new elements, accessories and colours. The City Park Café is a favourite hangout for all of the girls and the only set to include Marie (in pink).

**The café** served everything from burgers to freshly-baked cupcakes and pie.

## INVENTION LAB

3933 Olivia's Invention Workshop (2012)

Each of the friends has her own personality and interests. Olivia loves science, nature and inventions, so her workshop is full of tools, collection jars and even a microscope — not to mention her custom-built robot.

**LEGO Friends mini-dolls** have jointed heads, shoulders and single-piece legs to let them sit or stand.

**Emma (with black hair)** wants to be a clothing and jewellery designer. She's also into interior decorating, horseback riding and martial arts.

3187 Butterfly Beauty Shop (2012)

## BEAUTY SHOP

This salon at the centre of Heartlake City comes stocked with a variety of bows and clips that can be attached to mini-doll hair, as well as lipsticks, sunglasses and a hairdryer. It even has a fashion head display with a spare hair piece for the ultimate makeover.

## OLIVIA'S HOUSE

Along with her lab and tree house, Olivia comes in the biggest set in the theme's first year: the house where she lived with her parents and pet cat. Complete with a kitchen, bathroom, lounge, bedroom and rooftop patio, the house also included her mum Anna and dad Peter – the first male mini-doll figure.

Rooftop patio

Olivia keeps her diary in her bedroom drawer

**Olivia's house** is built in sections so that it can easily be taken apart and rearranged to make custom play-house creations.

Anna

Pete on turning chair

3315 Olivia's House (2012)

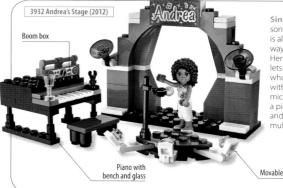

**The front yard** had a postbox, vegetable garden, lawnmower, swing set and an outdoor grill for barbecues with friends and family.

3932 Andrea's Stage (2012)

Boom box

**Singer** and song-writer Andrea is already on her way to being a star. Her music stage lets her put on a whole performance with the help of a microphone stand, a piano, a boom box and an entrance with multicoloured "lights".

Piano with bench and glass

Movable stage light

### ROAD TRIP

Stephanie's car was built just like any other LEGO vehicle, but in colours that delivered on many girls' preferences. It came with her puppy Coco, a carwash stand with a lamp-post, faucet and bucket and even a tiny MP3 player printed on a LEGO tile.

3183 Stephanie's Cool Convertible (2012)

3942 Heartlake Dog Show (2012)

### PET PARADE

The Heartlake Dog Show featured a podium with a runway, a canine obstacle course with a see-saw and hurdle, a grooming station, prize ribbons and a trophy for the winning pooch. It also had a plate of bones and a camera for snapping photos of well-trained pets.

**Mia loves** animals, whether training them or fixing them up when they're not feeling well.

# It's a LEGO® DUPLO® World!

**THE MOST WELL KNOWN** and enduring of the LEGO® construction systems for younger builders, LEGO® DUPLO® sets have bigger pieces that are easy for small fingers to handle, assemble and take apart. Designed for children between 1½ and 6 years old, these sets have been inspiring preschool creativity and helping children to develop early motor skills for more than 40 years ●

2940 Fire Truck (1992)

Standard 2x4 LEGO System brick

## THE LEGO DUPLO BRICK

The LEGO DUPLO brick is twice as tall, twice as long and twice as wide as a LEGO brick. The earliest DUPLO elements produced in 1969 had shorter studs and slightly different connectors underneath, but just like the modern version, they were fully compatible with standard LEGO pieces.

## TOOLS FOR TOTS

For preschoolers who wanted to use tools just like their parents, the DUPLO TOOLO sets of the 1990s had vehicles with yellow connection joints that could be locked or unlocked with play tools that made satisfying clicking sounds when turned. In 2009, the building system returned with brand-new sets featuring the same beloved, child-safe screwdrivers and wrenches.

## JUST IMAGINE...

DUPLO pieces with special shapes, colours and painted decorations mean that toddlers can build just about anything they can imagine, from buildings to animals to vehicles that float, roll and fly.

LOGO (1978)

## LOGO

The DUPLO rabbit was first used on packaging in 1979. In 1997, it was redesigned with a friendlier appearance to match the new PRIMO elephant logo for infant toys. It disappeared in 2002, when DUPLO was merged into the new LEGO Explore theme for young children, but returned when the DUPLO name appeared once again in 2004.

**The second rabbit** logo was designed to be cute, colourful and make eye contact with the viewer.

LOGO (1997)

LOGO (2014)

**The third DUPLO rabbit** hopped onto packaging in 2014. The latest DUPLO design is now paired with the classic LEGO logo.

## FIRST FIGURES

The DUPLO name did not always appear on young-builder packaging during the 1970s. Some boxes were labeled PreSchool, and others had no secondary title at all. This is when the first preschool human and animal figures were introduced, with decorated faces and simple, single-piece bodies.

537 Mary's House (1977)

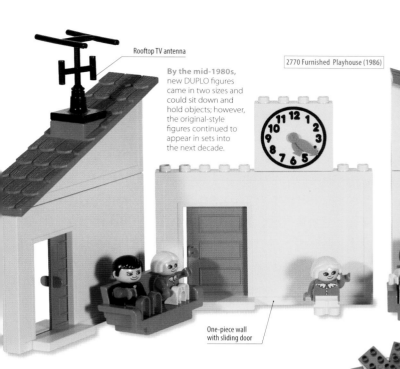

Rooftop TV antenna

By the mid-1980s, new DUPLO figures came in two sizes and could sit down and hold objects; however, the original-style figures continued to appear in sets into the next decade.

2770 Furnished Playhouse (1986)

One-piece wall with sliding door

## LEGO DUPLO PLAYHOUSE

In 1986, a DUPLO playhouse building set was released, featuring an assortment of family characters and furniture that could be used to assemble the interior of a rebuildable home. Separate accessory sets included parts for a bathroom, kitchen, lounge and extra wall and roof pieces. The concept would be visited again for several years during the 1990s.

## A DAY AT THE ZOO

Everybody knows that kids love animals. That's why the DUPLO Zoo theme has returned over and over again with sets full of vehicles, environments and lots of baby and grown-up animals.

A selection of animals and chararacters from various 1990s Zoo sets.

This stretched-out pooch doesn't just carry bricks. Thanks to its collar, it can connect to them too!

5503 DUPLO® Dog (2005)

## BRICK COLLECTIONS

As a toddler grows, so does his or her DUPLO brick collection. Parents can get extra pieces in a variety of handy storage containers, from sturdy plastic buckets to this friendly dachshund storage tube that came with 32 bricks inside its see-through cylinder body.

All aboard for the big top!

## LEGO DUPLO TRAINS

Another recurring favourite is DUPLO trains, which have their own track system and have been around since 2700 Preschool Freight Train in 1983. Built from 12 pieces, this circus train from the LEGO Ville daily life series had wheels with pistons that really moved when you pushed it forwards, the latest style of DUPLO figure and a baby elephant to ride in the back.

3770 My First Train (2005)

2024 Rattle (1983)

# Bricks for Baby

**THERE HAVE BEEN** many LEGO® products designed for younger children, from infants and toddlers to preschoolers almost ready to start building with LEGO® DUPLO® bricks. Some of these baby-safe building and learning toys were experiments that came and went quickly, while others were popular enough to be revisited again and again with different names and colours. Here are just a few of the LEGO items that the smallest builders have played and developed creativity with over the years ●

## SHAKE, RATTLE AND CHEW

This duck rattle may look simple, but it was the result of years of research on how babies play and learn. Because infants instinctively react to a moving eye, the duck's eyes bounced when the rattle was shaken and the ball in the middle could spin and make sounds. The two grips were added on the advice of a panel of mothers. Studs on top and openings on the bottom allowed the rattle to be attached to a child's DUPLO or LEGO bricks later on.

## BABY BRICKS

Colourful LEGO PRIMO and LEGO Baby pieces were made to be safe, sturdy and simple enough for the smallest builders to stack up and take apart.

Pieces from 5461 Shape Sorter House (2005)

## LEGO PRIMO & LEGO BABY

In 1995, the company unveiled LEGO PRIMO, a line of building toys with big, teething-proof pieces for babies between the ages of six and 24 months. In 1997, it became its own brand as LEGO PRIMO, with a yellow elephant logo and sets that included a shape sorter, a music-making boat, a buildable mouse and lots of colourful, durable, stackable pieces. PRIMO was renamed LEGO Baby in 2000, merged into LEGO Explore in 2002, became Baby again with a new teddy bear logo in 2004, and was officially discontinued in 2006.

2503 Musical Apple (2000)

**Pushing down** on the worm in the apple made it pop up and play music.

## BOUNCING BUG

A favourite of children aged six to 18 months all over the world, the Bendy Caterpillar would flatten out when pushed down, then spring up again when released for a guaranteed baby laugh. It could also roll around on the floor and came with bug friends that could be stacked up on the bumps on its back.

**The caterpillar** was also made in dark green and red for LEGO PRIMO in 1997 and yellow and dark green for LEGO Baby in 2001 and LEGO Explore in 2002.

5443 Hanging Rattle (2003)

## FOR THE YOUNGEST

This smiling-faced LEGO Explore rattle with fabric, string and soft plastic parts could hang from the railing of a crib or playpen. It was made for newborns under the "Explore Being Me" label.

5465 Bendy Caterpillar (2005)

5470 My First QUATRO Figure Set (2006)

**Less than** a dozen sets were released between 2004 and 2006, making this not just the first, but the only QUATRO figure ever made.

## LEGO® QUATRO™ THEME

As DUPLO bricks were to System bricks, so LEGO® QUATRO™ was to LEGO DUPLO. Made for children aged one to three, its teething-friendly pieces were more rounded and twice as long, wide and tall as the DUPLO versions. Emblazoned with a blue version of the original PRIMO elephant logo, QUATRO sets were mostly brick collections that focused more on building giant free-form towers than assembling models.

## MUSICAL CUTHBERT AND FRIEND

A LEGO PRIMO set for babies aged 0 to 2, Cuthbert the Camel was a music box that children could twist around to wind up and release to make him play a happy, soothing tune. His feet could attach to PRIMO pieces, and his hump was a stud that other compatible elements, including his round-bodied PRIMO figure friend, could stack on top of.

2007 Musical Cuthbert and Friend (1998)

## SHAPES & COLOURS

Released in the first year of the PRIMO brand after it was split off from the DUPLO one, this set helped babies aged eight to 24 months learn shapes and colours by discovering which pieces fit into which cubes. The cubes could be stacked on top of each other as well as on the green baseplate that served as the packaging lid.

2099 Shape Sorter (1997)

Train cars with bumps for stacking

2974 Play Train (2001)

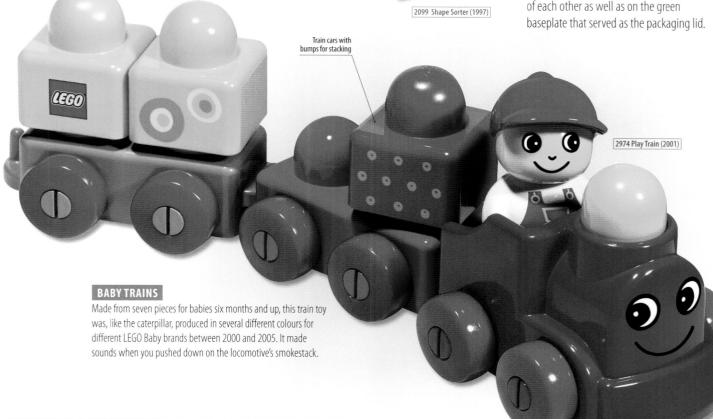

## BABY TRAINS

Made from seven pieces for babies six months and up, this train toy was, like the caterpillar, produced in several different colours for different LEGO Baby brands between 2000 and 2005. It made sounds when you pushed down on the locomotive's smokestack.

# Special Edition Sets

**THE MODELS** on these pages are all special editions, some created for milestone anniversaries, others to thrill the most experienced builders and some just to look good. If you have any of them in your collection, consider yourself one lucky LEGO® fan ●

**3443  LEGO Mosaic (2000)**

**Sold directly** from the LEGO website between 2000 and 2005, LEGO Mosaic let builders use the online Brick-o-Lizer to transform their own photographs into step-by-step instructions for assembling mosaics out of thousands of black, white and grey LEGO pieces.

Rotating turbine

**4999 Vestas Wind Turbine (2008)**

**This huge working windmill** was available only to employees of the Vestas company. More than 66cm (26in) high and built from nearly 800 pieces, the authentic reproduction towered over the tiny house and hill below.

**21001 John Hancock Tower (2008)**

**The LEGO** Architecture series debuted in 2008 with a series of desktop-sized miniature models of famous buildings from all around the world. Each licenced microscale replica includes a booklet full of facts and information about the history of the real building.

**21002 Empire State Building (2009)**

**21003 Seattle Space Needle (2009)**

**21000 Willis Tower (2008)**

Base with printed building name

**21012 Sydney Opera House™ (2012)**

**Australia's celebrated** Sydney Opera House (appropriately conceived by a Danish architect!) was built on a base of tan bricks, with white pieces used to make its interlocking vaulted shells.

**21010 Robie™ House (2011)**

**More than** 42cm (16.5in) wide and 13cm (5in) tall, this model used more than 2,000 small LEGO elements to recreate the landmark Prairie-style house built by Frank Lloyd Wright in Chicago.

**9247 Community Workers (2006)**

**Released in 2005** and revised in 2006 with different pieces and faces, this LEGO Education set contained a whole town's worth of 31 minifigures with accessories, including policemen, firefighters, construction workers, doctors, civilians and more.

**A LEGO Power Functions** motor (with a team of Vestas minifigures to keep it maintained) made the windmill spin and turned on lights in the house at its base.

White snow tiles

Street light

Light-up house

Maintenance van

**The third** of the Winter Village sets featured a small-town post office with postal workers, an old-time mail truck with gifts, a pavilion for musicians and a couple of kids having a snowball fight.

**10222 Winter Village Post Office (2011)**

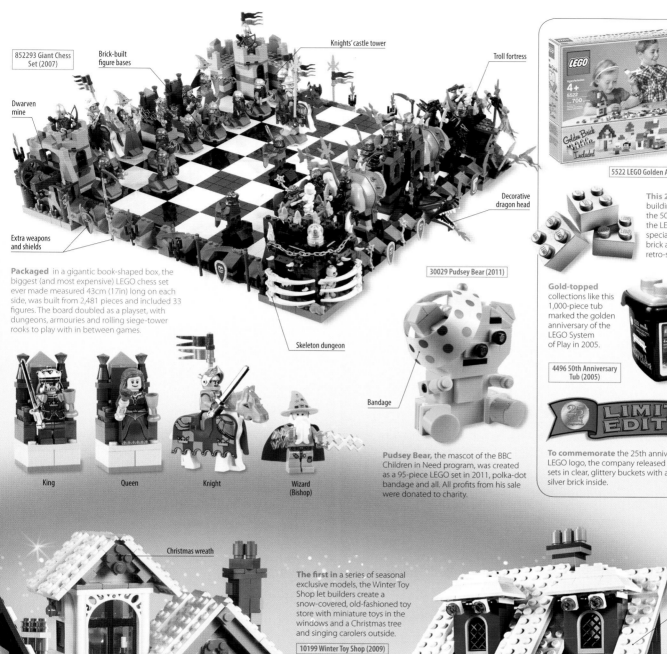

852293 Giant Chess Set (2007)

Brick-built figure bases

Knights' castle tower

Troll fortress

Dwarven mine

Extra weapons and shields

Decorative dragon head

**Packaged** in a gigantic book-shaped box, the biggest (and most expensive) LEGO chess set ever made measured 43cm (17in) long on each side, was built from 2,481 pieces and included 33 figures. The board doubled as a playset, with dungeons, armouries and rolling siege-tower rooks to play with in between games.

Skeleton dungeon

King

Queen

Knight

Wizard (Bishop)

30029 Pudsey Bear (2011)

Bandage

**Pudsey Bear,** the mascot of the BBC Children in Need program, was created as a 95-piece LEGO set in 2011, polka-dot bandage and all. All profits from his sale were donated to charity.

5522 LEGO Golden Anniversary Set (2008)

**This 2008** creative building set celebrated the 50th anniversary of the LEGO brick with a special-edition golden brick and classic retro-style packaging.

**Gold-topped** collections like this 1,000-piece tub marked the golden anniversary of the LEGO System of Play in 2005.

4496 50th Anniversary Tub (2005)

**To commemorate** the 25th anniversary of the LEGO logo, the company released limited-edition sets in clear, glittery buckets with an exclusive silver brick inside.

Christmas wreath

**The first in** a series of seasonal exclusive models, the Winter Toy Shop let builders create a snow-covered, old-fashioned toy store with miniature toys in the windows and a Christmas tree and singing carolers outside.

10199 Winter Toy Shop (2009)

Snowy roof plates

Bakery shop sign

**The Winter Village** theme continued with a cosy bakery full of treats for a frosty day. It also had a tree-seller's stand and cart and a frozen pond for ice skaters.

10216 Winter Village Bakery (2010)

# MEET THE MINIGFIGURES

You don't have to be tall to make history. Gandhi was 5'3", Beethoven was 5'3¾" and Picasso was 5'4". Between them they led India to independence, wrote the Fifth Symphony and co-founded the Cubist movement. Well, the LEGO® minifigure has them all beat. At only 1½ inches tall, it is the shortest superstar of all time. For more than 30 years, the minifigure has made it possible for children to populate their LEGO worlds with a diverse cast of characters, from pirates and soldiers to deep-sea divers and aliens. The minifigure has also become an icon that defies cultural boundaries and generational divides, consistently standing small as one of the most revolutionary and popular toys of all time.

The first minifigures in 1978 were based on archetypal characters such as spacemen, policemen, nurses and knights and were facially identical – yellow skin, two black dots for eyes and a wide smile – in order to represent people from anywhere in the world. But a lot has changed over the years. In 2003, minifigures were given realistic skin tones, facial expressions and moulded hair when they represented real people or named characters from movies or TV series – starting with LEGO Basketball minifigures and continuing with the licenced series.

Spaceman • 1979

# BRINGING LEGO®
# PLAY TO LIFE

**IN THE 1960s** and early 1970s, the focus in LEGO® building was on constructing models like houses, cars and trains. But something important was missing: people to live in the houses, drive the cars and run the trains! If children wanted characters to play in their LEGO creations, they had to make them out of bricks themselves. To address this need for role-play and storytelling, the company first created large, buildable family figures, and later shrunk them down to a size that would fit in better with smaller LEGO models. In1975, a figure was launched with a blank yellow head, a torso with arm-shaped bumps and a single, solid leg. In 1978, this forerunner to the minifigure was updated with moving arms and legs, hands that could hold accessories and a face painted with two dots for eyes and a friendly smile. The famous LEGO minifigure was ready to play!

**Minifigure patent** The 1979 US patent for the LEGO minifigure design demonstrated its iconic shape, the brick-compatible holes on its feet and legs and the way its limbs could move.

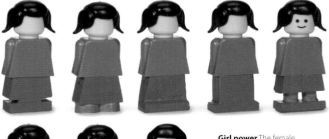

**Girl power** The female minifigure went through many concept stages before it was decided that it would share the same standard legs as male minifigures.

## BIRTH OF A LEGEND

To create the prototype for the first minifigure, designer Jens Nygård Knudsen and a team of colleagues sawed and filed LEGO bricks into a miniature human form. Three years and 50 additional prototypes carved in plastic and cast in tin later, he produced the updated modern-style minifigure. It debuted in set number 600, featuring a policeman and a buildable brick patrol car.

**LEGO Family**
A best-selling precursor to the minifigure, the first LEGO Family figures appeared in 1974 in set 200. The set included five family members with posable arms, brick-built bodies, and swappable reversible hair pieces.

## MINI-EVOLUTION
As behind-the-scenes development progressed, the minifigure gained separated legs, multiple moving parts and a decorated face. Common to all was the stud on top of the head, which allowed a variety of hats and hair elements to be attached, thereby creating different personalities and jobs – and endless imaginative play opportunities for children.

This early minifigure was the version launched in 1975.

Ring-shaped hands . . . . . . . .

Hat compatible with modern-style minifigures . . . . . . . . .

An experiment in hinged legs

Arms can swing back and forth . . . . .

Hollow legs and feet fit over LEGO brick studs

**Then and now**
The 1978 minifigures, seen here, were essentially the same as the ones that can be found in LEGO sets today.

Head concept with sculpted features . . . . . . . . . .

Hand-drawn prototype torso decoration . . . . . . . . .

# WHAT'S A MINIFIGURE?

**Size matters** Without a hat or hair piece, a minifigure stands exactly four LEGO bricks high. This precise measurement makes it easy to construct LEGO buildings and vehicles that can fit minifigures inside.

**A LEGO® MINIFIGURE** is a small, posable figure of a person or being. Most minifigures have rotating arms, legs, hands and heads. They have connectors on their bodies that are compatible with LEGO bricks and other elements. They often represent famous archetypes, such as firefighters, astronauts and knights. A minifigure can be disassembled and combined with parts from other minifigures to create an entirely new character. The faces of many minifigures carry a friendly smile, but some have other expressions – even multiple ones! Minifigures drive cars, live in castles, fly spaceships and fill the world of construction with endless possibilities for fun, role play and imagination.

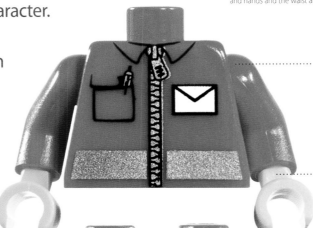

Stud on top of head can connect to headgear and other LEGO pieces

**Build a minifigure**
A standard LEGO minifigure comes in three sections when you open a new LEGO set: the head, the torso with arms and hands and the waist and legs.

Arm rotates 360 degrees at the shoulder

Hand swivels at the wrist

Legs swing back and forth for sitting and walking poses

Holes on backs of legs and bottoms of feet attach to LEGO brick studs

## MINIFIGURES AT WORK

LEGO minifigures hail from many different places and times, including the past, present and future, as well as worlds of fantasy and science fiction. You can tell where a minifigure comes from and what kind of job it has by looking at the details of its printed clothing and its accessories.

A uniform with reflective stripes and a special helmet make it clear that this is a firefighter.

With his overalls, cap and shovel, what else could this hard-working fellow be but a farmer?

An ancient gladiator carries a sword and shield, and wears a protective helmet and leather armour.

## MEET THE MINIFIGURES...

A minifigure must have a number of essential key minifigure characteristics in order to be considered a true LEGO minifigure. Although all of the characters shown here have different faces, clothes, accessories and even some body parts, each one is still a minifigure because it is based around the same basic LEGO minifigure design.

The pirate has a hook-hand, a peg-leg and a printed eyepatch and beard.

This retro robot has a mechanical arm with a claw, a helmet with a visor and bolts printed on his body and legs.

This mermaid stands on a single-piece fish tail instead of legs.

A queen from LEGO® Castle wears a dress made from a printed sloped piece.

A beastly warrior has an animal head with a reversible minifigure face underneath.

This cheerleader has legs that are printed to look like a skirt and socks.

Some minifigures have short legs to make them appear smaller.

The EXO-FORCE™ heroes are based on the look of Japanese animation.

Minifigures can represent anybody from any country or culture.

**Handy** A zookeeper holds a banana in one hand and a hungry baby chimpanzee in the other.

### HAIR, HATS AND GEAR
The minifigure's head stud lets you attach and swap hundreds of different hair pieces, hats and helmets. Their hands can hold a wide variety of accessories, and backpacks and armour can be attached to their bodies.

**Armour** This knight wears a helmet and an armour piece fitted over his torso.

# MEET THE NON-MINIFIGURES...

Not every LEGO figure is a minifigure! Though they are small, many other characters inhabit the universe of LEGO building. The LEGO® Friends mini-doll is not a minifigure because it is not made up of any standard minifigure parts. The skeleton does not have enough standard parts to be a true minifigure. The Jay Microfigure is only half as tall as a minifigure.

**LEGO skeleton**

**Jay Microfigure**

**LEGO Friends mini-doll**

# HOW IS A MINIFIGURE MADE?

Many minifigures start out as a rough concept sketch that shows how the character might appear when it's created.

**CREATING A NEW MINIFIGURE** isn't a quick process. It can take more than a year from the time an idea is first sketched out on paper to the moment a brand-new plastic character is picked off the LEGO® production line to be packed up and shipped to shops all around the world. Many individuals contribute to the creation of a minifigure, from sculptors to graphic artists, as well as the machines that make sure each one is perfectly moulded and ready for play. Here's how it's done.

The LEGO Minifigures team hold brainstorming sessions at the LEGO offices in Billund, Denmark.

## BRAINSTORMING

When it's time to start work on new sets for a LEGO play theme, the whole design team sits down for a "Design Boost" brainstorming session. They share their ideas to come up with the best concepts for new models and the minifigures that will populate them. If a new set will need one or more new minifigures to be created, then the character design process begins.

# DESIGNING

The design team makes sketches and decides what new accessories or body-part elements are needed. For research, they might visit a fire station, or study historical armour at a library. Element designers hand-sculpt organic-looking pieces such as hair at a 3:1 scale out of clay, while more regularly shaped parts are designed via a computer using a 3D program. Meanwhile, graphic designers create a map of face and body details that will be applied to the minifigure.

Minifigures are chosen to be included in a set based on how well they help to tell that set's story. If it is a licenced character from a movie or comic book, then the team collaborates with licensing partners until both are totally satisfied with the design. Finally, a Model Committee checks that everything fits and works properly, and the completed design is approved for production.

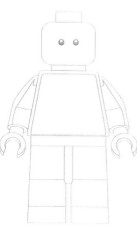

Design work begins on a blank minifigure template, bare of any colours, personality or details.

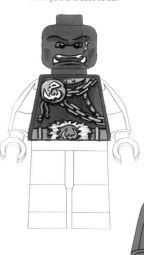

A graphic designer comes up with a design for the face and costume of the new minifigure and adds colour.

The approved design is refined and finalised on a computer as a 2D version of what the minifigure will look like when it is produced in plastic.

Most minifigures are manufactured at the LEGO Group headquarters in Billund, Denmark. Others come from factories in Hungary, the Czech Republic, China and Mexico.

# MANUFACTURING

Just like LEGO bricks, minifigures start out as piles of tiny, colourful plastic granules, made out of acrylonitrile butadiene styrene (ABS), each one about the size of a grain of rice. These granules are mixed together and heated until they melt and become a plastic goo, which is pressed into shape inside metal moulding machines. Automated assembly machines attach legs to waists, hands to arms, and arms to torsos. Decorating machines then use special inks to print faces and clothing decorations directly onto the assembled parts. At last, the new minifigure is complete and ready to be purchased, shipped and sold.

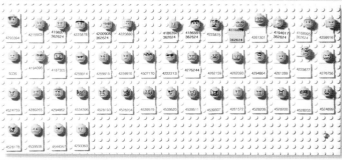

The LEGO employees at the factories use coded display boards to keep track of the many different minifigure faces that are currently in production.

# TIMELINE

**EVEN THOUGH** their fundamental design has remained the same for more than 35 years, minifigures have gone through many changes over the decades. This timeline chronicles some of the most important events in minifigure history, including the first new facial expressions and new body parts and the first licenced characters from the big screen, as well as the debuts of classic minifigure elements, accessories and other LEGO® figures.

LEGO Family figures

### 1974
- The first LEGO figures – LEGO Family building figures – have round heads with painted expressions, posable arms and bodies built out of LEGO bricks.

Freddy Fox LEGO FABULAND figure

Handy briefcase to carry everything a minifigure needs

Castle horse has space for rider to slot in

### 1979
- First yellow Space minifigure.
- First female Castle character.
- First male hair piece. • First chef's hat. •
Animal-headed LEGO® FABULAND™ figures.

### 1980
- First top hat.

### 1983
- First minifigure briefcase.

### 1984
- New Castle factions and elements are introduced.
- Minifigure-rideable horse.

Monkey figure with curly tail

### 1989
- LEGO® Pirates introduces the first minifigures with different facial expressions and body parts, such as peg-legs and hook-hands.
- Monkey uses minifigure arms for all four limbs.

### 1990
- The first LEGO ghost minifigure has a glow-in-the-dark shroud element.
- First time a slope is used instead of legs for a minifigure's dress.

LEGO DUPLO figures

Early three-piece figure with red hat

## 1975

- Small and simple three-piece LEGO figures are released, with an unpainted face and no separate limbs. ● First minifigure-compatible headgear.

## 1976

- LEGO® DUPLO® figures are launched.

## 1978

- The first true LEGO minifigure, with posable arms and legs and the classic smile expression. ● The LEGOLAND® subthemes Town, Castle and Space launch with new minifigure accessories and wearable gear.

LEGO Technic figure

## 1985

- Record number of new Town minifigures are released.● New Space jetpack with stud on the front accessory.

## 1986

- LEGO® Technic figure is launched.● New Castle maiden hat.

## 1987

- New Forestman cap.

LEGO BELVILLE figures

## 1992

- First minifigure head with freckles.
- New surfboard accessory.

## 1993

- First female LEGO Space minifigure.
- First separate beard piece. ● First minifigure headgear with printing. ● First LEGO Town crook. ● First fabric minifigure cape.

## 1994

- First printed minifigure legs.
- First robot minifigure head.
- LEGO® BELVILLE™ figures are launched.

LEGO® *Island* video game

### 1995

● First skeleton figure has new body and limb components. ● New diver accessories: helmet, visor and flippers. ● First minifigure crown.

### 1996

● First minifigure nose.

### 1997

● First minifigure with a printed sloped skirt piece. ● LEGO *Island* is the first video game to star (digital) minifigures. ● LEGO® SCALA™ figures are launched.

### 2001

● LEGO® Alpha Team Dash Justice minifigure.

### 2002

● First minifigures to feature new short LEGO leg piece. ● First super hero minifigure. ● LEGO® Studios werewolf mask transforms an ordinary minifigure into a howling beast. ● Neck bracket element allows objects to be attached to a minifigure's back.

### 2003

● LEGO® Adventurers introduces new Sherpa hat. ● First minifigures based on actual people – with realistic skin tones. ● First minifigure with arm printing. ● The first minifigures on Mars – illustrations of astrobots Biff Starling and Sandy Moondust land on the Red Planet aboard the NASA rovers *Spirit* and *Opportunity*.

### 2005

● Minifigures with in-built batteries let Jedi lightsabers and police flashlights light up when the heads are pushed down. ● Hand-held magnetic accessory lets Harry Potter™ grab a golden dragon egg. ● First minifigure mermaid tail. ● First viking helmet.

Brightly coloured LEGO® Games microfigures

### 2009

● Tiny microfigures appear in LEGO Games sets. ● LEGO® Space Police features new modified alien heads. ● First hair piece with a hole for accessories.

### 2010

● LEGO® *Toy Story*™ sets introduce minifigures with extra-long arms and legs. ● A new tentacle-legs element first appears in LEGO® Atlantis. ● Han Solo (from LEGO *Star Wars*) is the first minifigure to be frozen in carbonite. ● The collectible LEGO Minifigures line adds many new body parts and accessories. ● First minifigure legs with side printing. ● *The Adventures of Clutch Powers* is the first feature-length movie starring minifigures.

## 1998

- LEGO® Adventurers introduces new headgear: wide-brimmed hat, pith helmet and aviator cap with goggles. ● LEGO Castle's Ninja subtheme launches Samurai and ninja gear.
- First mummy minifigure.

## 1999

- LEGO® *Star Wars*™ minifigures introduce many new parts and accessories.
- First minifigure head to be sculpted into a different (non-standard) shape.

## 2000

- LEGO® Studios Director minifigure.

Skeleton figure with sword

Giant Troll figure

## 2006

- LEGO® EXO-FORCE™ features minifigures with faces and hair pieces designed after Japanese animation, as well as robot villains with new body, arm and leg pieces. ● First printed hair piece.

## 2007

- LEGO® Castle launches new armour parts. ● Skeleton minifigure body is updated so its arms can move.
- LEGO® Mars Mission features aliens with transparent glow-in-the-dark bodies.
- First minifigures with soft-plastic heads.

## 2008

- "Go Miniman Go!" event celebrates the 30th anniversary of the LEGO minifigure.
- LEGO® Agents introduces a new robotic minifigure arm.
- The Castle theme introduces the Giant Troll figure.

Frakjaw from LEGO® Ninjago

Meet mini-doll Nicole from LEGO Friends

## 2011

- Aluminium minifigures of the Roman gods Jupiter and Juno and the astronomer Galileo are launched aboard the Juno space probe. ● A new leg piece gives boots to LEGO Ninjago skeleton figures. ● First hair piece with ears.

## 2012

- LEGO Ninjago introduces snake head and tail pieces and a torso extender with extra arms.
- LEGO® Friends debuts the mini-doll.
- LEGO® Monster Fighters features new bat-winged arms and steampunk mechanical leg pieces.

## 2013

- First minifigure with chicken wings.
- New animal minifigure elements in LEGO® Legends of Chima™.
- New heads and turtle shells for the LEGO® Teenage Mutant Ninja Turtles™.

## 2014

- The incredibly successful *The Lego Movie* is released. Many minifigure parts debut in the film's themed sets.
- The LEGO® Mixels are launched.

# GOOD VS BAD

**HEROES, IT IS SAID,** are measured by the villains they battle. If that's the case, LEGO® minifigure heroes have nothing to worry about, for they have faced some of the most formidable villains in the history of toys. From the Black Falcon knights and the Space Police's most wanted aliens, to Captain Brickbeard and Lord Vampyre, all the way up to infamous types such as Lord Garmadon and Cragger, the roster of minifigure evildoers is long and colourful. Fortunately, for every bad guy there is a brave hero or heroine ready to fight for justice!

**Castle** They look peaceful enough now, but the Crusaders and the Black Falcons fought against each other for eight years.

**LEGO Monster Fighters** Finally, Major Quinton Steele has got his hands on a moonstone. But with the Werewolf in hot pursuit, he had better run as fast as his minifigure legs can carry him!

**LEGO Ninjago** If anyone can take on the evil Lord Garmadon and win, it's the Ultimate Spinjitzu Master, Lloyd Garmadon!

**LEGO Space Police III** The Space Police work hard to protect the minifigure public from hardened alien criminals such as leader of the Space Biker Gang, Kranxx.

**LEGO Agents** Agent Trace isn't intimidated by Fire Arm's massive gun – but she is offended by his flat-top hair piece.

**LEGO Monster Fighters** Lord Vampyre plans to inflict darkness upon the world. His archenemy Dr Rodney Rathbone does all he can to stop him.

**LEGO Pirates** Captain Redbeard sails the seas in search of treasure, trying to avoid Governor Broadside and his Imperial Officers.

**LEGO Atlantis** Ace Speedman searches for the lost city of Atlantis, but this Shark Warrior isn't going to give it up easily.

**LEGO Agents** Agent Chase has to stop Dr Inferno – not only does he plan to take over the world, but his hair piece is a crime against fashion.

**LEGO Alien Conquest** The Aliens landed on Earth to collect brainpower from humans, but come up against the Alien Defence Unit Sergeant and his team.

## LEGO Legends of Chima
Cragger and Prince of the Lion Tribe Laval used to be best friends. But once Cragger discovers the power of CHI, it signals the end of their friendship and of Chima's Age of Peace.

## LEGO Legends of Chima
Determined to ensure CHI is distributed fairly, laidback Gorilla Grizzam better watch out for wicked Wilhurt!

**Castle** When the Crusaders aren't battling the Black Falcons, they have to contend with the Forestmen.

## LEGO Ninjago
Spitta goes after Sensei Wu with his mace. He's in for a shock when he discovers that the wise Sensei is a Spinjitzu Master.

## LEGO CITY
The sneaky crook gets up to mischief in LEGO CITY, but the Policeman always manages to catch him.

**LEGO Atlantis** Even though the mighty Portal Emperor is in front of him greedily guarding sunken treasure, Lance Spears doesn't look perturbed.

**Seagull** The Sea Captain's faithful friend perches on his hand when it wants a rest.

**Chainsaw** Razar the Raven's weapon is a mighty sight to behold. The chainsaw is spiked with Crocodile teeth. Ouch!

**Frying pan** Watch out! The Governor's Daughter is wielding a big silver frying pan and she looks pretty mad!

**Maracas** It's party time! Clip on the Maraca Man's colourful maracas and watch him shake them to the beat.

**Backpack** The brown pack loops around Sangye Dorje's neck, and has a handy pickaxe holder on the side. Snow shoes also help the Sherpa to cross the mountains.

**Briefcase and ticket** This Passenger minifigure looks business-like with his briefcase accessory. Clip his ticket to his hand and off he goes to board the train.

# MINI GEAR

**MINIFIGURES WERE** given C-shaped hands so they could carry things – and boy, have they ever carried things! LEGO® minifigure gear can be practical, such as a sword for defending the king's treasure or a tool used on the job, or just fun, such as a piece of sports equipment or a magic wand. The kind of gear they carry helps to distinguish one minifigure from another and is great for role play. For example, the crook might have the stolen money in his hand but the police officer is ready for him with the handcuffs! Watch for new gear every year.

**Money** There's a sinister squid on the loose! The Squidman minifigure flees the scene of the crime, carrying his stolen loot in his hand.

**Pom-poms**
The Cheerleader's hands fit securely inside her blue and white pom-poms.

**Handcart** The Railway Employee minifigure transports the passengers' luggage. He doesn't look very thrilled about it!

**Parrot** Pieces of eight! Every good pirate needs a parrot pal.

**Sword**
LEGO Ninjago's Cole minifigure clutches tightly to the engraved hilt of his long katana sword.

**Tarot cards** The Fortune Teller is never seen without her trusty tarot cards. Printed on 1x2 tiles, one shows the sun and the other a tower.

**Magic wand** Abracadabra! Clip the Magician's wand into his hand and he's ready to conjure up a spell.

**Tools** The Harbour Worker is a busy man, but luckily tools like his handy spanner and mallet make life a little easier.

**Trophy** The Karate Master carries a golden miniature minifigure statuette. The perfect prize!

**Paintbrush and palette**
The Artist's paint-splattered palette and brush accessories were brand new for 2011.

**Steak and cleaver**
The Butcher's T-bone steak has a bone to make it easier to hold. The big cleaver and steak were brand-new accessories.

**Pistols**
Frank Rock from LEGO Monster Fighters is a great shot with his twin silver pistols.

**Police badge and handcuffs**
The Policeman's badge is printed on a 1x2 tile, like the Fortune Teller's tarot cards. His handcuffs have a cylinder-shaped piece for a firm grip.

# A CUT ABOVE

**THE FIRST MINIFIGURES** had very simple hairstyles, but as time has passed, hair pieces have gotten more varied and downright crazy! As with hats and other headgear, hair pieces attach to the stud on top of the head piece. Hair can help to identify a character – for example, everyone knows Princess Leia's two buns or Superman's forehead curl. Hair can also reflect the style of a theme, such as the LEGO® EXO-FORCE™ anime-inspired hair pieces. Some hair pieces include facial hair, such as Hagrid's bushy beard, the Caveman's moustache and many others. Pigtails, wigs and even mohawks – minifigures have had them all.

**Pigtails** · 1978 · Doctor · LEGOLAND Town.

**Short back and sides** · 1979 · Boy · LEGOLAND Town.

**Shaggy long hair and beard** · 2001 · Rubeus Hagrid · LEGO® Harry Potter™.

**Medium-length centre parting** · 2001 · Albus Dumbledore · LEGO Harry Potter.

**Flowing, swept back long hair** · 2007 · Crown Princess · LEGO Castle.

**Severe bob with a straight fringe** · 2008 · Claw-Dette · LEGO Agents.

**Shoulder-length, tousled** · 2010 · Caveman · LEGO Minifigures.

**Slick bob with gold hairband** · 2011 · Egyptian Queen · LEGO Minifigures.

**Smooth bun** · 2011 · Kimono Girl · LEGO Minifigures.

**Messy updo with bone hair band** · 2011 · Cave Woman · LEGO Minifigures.

**Upswept hair with bun** · 2011 · Ice Skater · LEGO Minifigures.

**Extra long, straight hair with hairband** · 2012 · Hippie · LEGO Minifigures.

**Messed-up bed hair** · 2012 · Sleepyhead · LEGO Minifigures.

**Swept fringe with headphones** · 2012 · DJ · LEGO Minifigures.

**Judge's wig** · 2013 · Judge · LEGO Minifigures.

**Combed short hair with gold leaves** · 2013 · Roman Emperor · LEGO Minifigures.

**Short bob cut, swept fringe**
• 1983 • Striped Lady
• LEGOLAND Town.

**Ponytail** • 1992 • Female Swimmer
• LEGO Paradisa.

**Long plaits with headband**
• 1997 • Plain Native American
• LEGO Western.

**Bun** • 1999 • Padmé Naberrie
• LEGO® Star Wars™.

**Side buns** • 2000 • Princess Leia
• LEGO Star Wars.

**Short bowl cut** • 2001
• Ron Weasley • LEGO Harry Potter.

**Combed widow's peak** • 2002
• Vampire • LEGO Studios.

**Half slicked back, half spiked**
• 2006 • Two Face • LEGO® Batman™.

**Futuristic hair with spikes
to the side** • 2006 • Hikaru
• LEGO EXO-FORCE.

**Floppy hair in angular sections**
• 2006 • Takeshi • LEGO EXO-FORCE.

**Floppy, flowing male hair**
• 2008 • Anakin Skywalker
• LEGO® Star Wars® Clone Wars™.

**Stripy, long head-tails with
twin peaks** • 2008 • Ahsoka Tano
• LEGO Star Wars Clone Wars.

**Stripy spikes** • 2008 • Dr Inferno
• LEGO Agents.

**Wavy updo** • 2009
• Nightclub Willie Scott
• LEGO® Indiana Jones™.

**Bubble perm** • 2010 • Circus Clown
• LEGO Minifigures.

**Mohawk spike** • 2011 • Punk Rocker
• LEGO Minifigures.

**Classic Superman with curl**
• 2011 • Superman
• LEGO® DC Universe™ Super Heroes.

**Swept back hair with attached
pointy ears** • 2011 • Elf
• LEGO Minifigures.

**High ponytail with pink stripe**
• 2012 • Skater Girl
• LEGO Minifigures.

**Long, layered bob** • 2012
• Rocker Girl • LEGO Minifigures.

**Hair plaited with strips of bark**
• 2013 • Forest Maiden
• LEGO Minifigures.

**Wavy retro bob** • 2013
• Hollywood Starlet
• LEGO Minifigures.

**Comb-over** • 2013 • Grandpa
• LEGO Minifigures.

**Tangled snakes** • 2013 • Medusa
• LEGO Minifigures.

**Sleek layered hair** • 2013
• Trendsetter • LEGO Minifigures.

# ON THE MOVE!

**THERE'S ONE THING** you can say about LEGO®
minifigures: they never stand still! Over the years,
minifigures have ridden just about every kind of vehicle
you can imagine, from skateboards and snowboards to
motorbikes and aeroplanes. Animals have helped get
them from place to place too, including elephants,
horses and even ostriches. But whatever they use,
whether it is wheeled, winged or on four
feet, minifigures travel all over the LEGO
world looking for adventure!

**Jetpack** Featuring twin handles, this
gadget is essential for the Blacktron II
Commander's adventures.

**Scooter** This happy little boy loves
rolling along on his push-scooter.

**Fairy wings** The dainty wings are
on a bracket around the Fairy's neck.

**Spinner**
The Green Ninja
minifigure swirls
up a tornado.
A unique green
crown fits on top
of the spinner.

**Skateboard** The minifigure's feet
clip onto the skateboard's studs.

**Roller skates** Roller Derby Girl zips
along on her detachable black wheels.

**Speedor** Worriz the Wolf's Speedor
wheel is strong, powerful and fast.

**Elephant and cart** Pippin the reporter enjoys the bumpy but scenic route from the cart as Babloo encourages his elephant on!

**Windsurfing**
The windsurfing minifigure clings on tightly to the boom. Life's a breeze, if he can keep his balance!

**Horse** This faithful steed is made from two LEGO pieces.

**Skis** Fix the studs on the skis to the Skier's feet and off he zooms.

**Snowboard**
This minifigure's snowboard is weighted to keep him upright and moving down the slope of his set, Snowboard Boarder Cross Race (3538).

**Spring-loaded legs**
In 2003, spring-loaded legs and special new arms were created, allowing this NBA Basketball player to slam dunk the ball.

**Bicycle** This bright red bicycle is the perfect transport for riding around town taking pictures.

**Flippers** These flippers are essential for exploring the depths of the ocean.

**Ice Skates** Wearing these detachable skates, the Ice Skater performs dazzling moves on the ice.

**Broomstick** Every witch knows that brooms are the best way to travel.

# A LEGO® World

**FROM INTERNATIONAL** fan clubs to action-packed video games, from minifigure movies to artists' studios, the LEGO® brick has definitely made the leap from simple plastic construction toy to global phenomenon. Every day, people around the world are finding new ways to move beyond the instruction booklets and make their passion for LEGO building a part of their lives. Read on to discover how some of them show off and share their love of imagination, creativity and that famous little brick ●

# LEGOLAND® PARKS

**LEGO® FANS** have always constructed their own LEGO worlds, but until the first LEGOLAND® theme park opened in Billund, Denmark, in 1968, they never had one big enough to walk around in! Today, LEGOLAND Parks, Discovery Centres, water parks and hotels can be found all around the world. Filled with the miniature cities and monuments of MINILAND, thrilling LEGO themed rides, enormous brick-built sculptures and spectacular, specially built models, they're both a fan and a family's dream come true ●

**A 2012 map of LEGOLAND® Billund** guides visitors to all of the theme park's areas and attractions, including MINILAND, Pirate Land, Adventure Land, the Imagination Zone, LEGOREDO® Town, the new Polar Land and much more.

# Park Design

**AS THE LEGO® BRICK'S** fame grew in the 1960s, so did the number of visitors to the company's Billund headquarters. When Godtfred Kirk Christiansen realised that more than 20,000 people a year were coming to admire the elaborate LEGO sculptures that decorated the factories, he decided to create an outdoor display. Envisioned as a small garden, it became the first ever LEGOLAND® Park ●

**THE FIRST PARK**

The original LEGOLAND Park opened on 7 June 1968 and quickly became Denmark's most popular tourist attraction outside its capital city, Copenhagen. It originally took up nearly 38,100 sq m (125,000 sq ft), but doubled in size over the next 30 years.

## PARKS AROUND THE WORLD

With the success of LEGOLAND® Billund came the idea to create more parks in other countries. LEGOLAND Parks opened in Windsor, UK, in 1996, followed by California, USA, in 1999, Günzburg, Germany, in 2002, Florida, USA, in 2011 and Malaysia in 2012.

Based on a LEGOLAND® Windsor model, these concept sketches depict a moving, water-shooting dinosaur sculpture designed for the main entrance at LEGOLAND® California.

Brick-built dinosaur sculpture

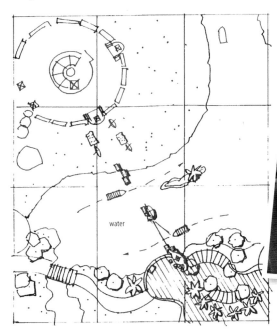

water

The final display closely resembles the concept artwork, except that the dinosaur construction worker has changed from green to red.

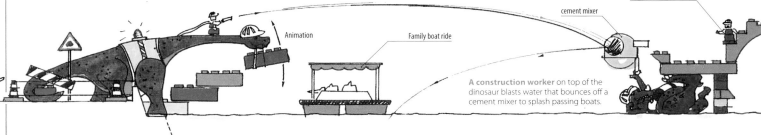

Animation

Family boat ride

cement mixer

Large-scale "minifigure"

A construction worker on top of the dinosaur blasts water that bounces off a cement mixer to splash passing boats.

## RIDES AND ATTRACTIONS

The LEGOLAND Parks are filled with constantly changing themed areas, interactive rides and seasonal events, from LEGOLAND Windsor's transport-themed Traffic section with its Driving School and Fire Academy rides, and the wild rides and coasters of LEGOLAND® California's Dino Island and Castle Hill, to LEGOLAND® Deutschland's Imagination area featuring the Build & Test Center, Kids' Power Tower and Pedal-A-Car ride.

**Each car** of the Pedal-A-Car attraction at LEGOLAND Deutschland holds four passengers.

**LEGOLAND® Malaysia** is the sixth LEGOLAND Park and the first to be built in Asia. Divided into seven themed areas, its 76 acres of adventure are packed full of more than 40 rides, shows and attractions.

**Under construction (left)**, the elevated ride track circles around LEGOLAND Deutschland's Imagination section, giving riders a spectacular view of the Park.

**As they pass** over MINILAND, Pedal-A-Car passengers can look down over a scale model of Bavaria's Neuschwanstein Castle built from more than 300,000 LEGO bricks.

LEGOLAND Deutschland model builders built a scale replica of Munich Airport entirely out of LEGO bricks!

## MAKING MODEL MAGIC

Around every corner of a LEGOLAND Park is an amazing LEGO sculpture. The Parks are home to thousands of models of buildings, people and animals, built from millions of LEGO bricks. Each LEGOLAND Park has its own team of model designers and builders who take care of the Park's existing sculptures and create all-new ones.

**A LEGOLAND** model builder assembles a 1:20-scale model of an Airbus A380 passenger airliner in the German Park's workshop.

**Finishing touches** are added on-site to LEGOLAND Deutschland's MINILAND Munich Airport display. Every morning, the model builders tour the Park to check, repair and clean all of its models.

# Allianz Arena

**PROUDLY DISPLAYED** in MINILAND at LEGOLAND® Deutschland in Günzburg, Germany, is the Allianz Arena, one of the biggest LEGO® buildings in the world. Constructed from more than a million LEGO bricks, the 1: 50-scale model of Munich's famous football stadium is 5m (16.5ft) long, 4.5m (15ft) wide and 1m (3.3ft) high, and weighs in at 1.4 tonnes (1.5 tons) ●

No pressure... I'm only being watched by 70,000 fans!

Special semi-translucent bricks let exterior glow

**Even at** its smaller than MINILAND-standard minifigure scale, the arena model is enormous next to a pair of LEGOLAND Deutschland's smaller visitors. Button controls on the nearby columns activate special moving features inside the model.

**When the sun sets** and night falls, 5,000 LEDs (Light-Emitting Diodes) illuminate the MINILAND Allianz Arena in red or blue to represent the colours of the Bayern Munich and 1860 Munich football teams – just like the real thing!

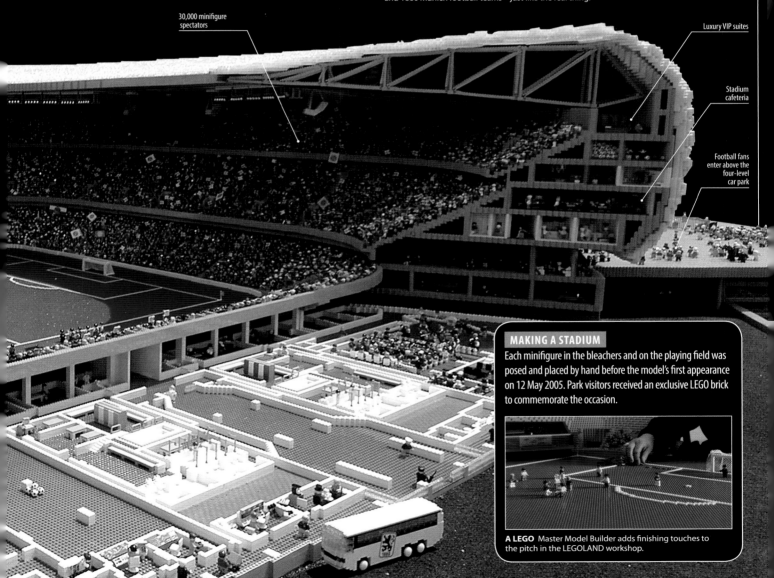

30,000 minifigure spectators

Luxury VIP suites

Stadium cafeteria

Football fans enter above the four-level car park

### MAKING A STADIUM

Each minifigure in the bleachers and on the playing field was posed and placed by hand before the model's first appearance on 12 May 2005. Park visitors received an exclusive LEGO brick to commemorate the occasion.

**A LEGO** Master Model Builder adds finishing touches to the pitch in the LEGOLAND workshop.

# MINILAND Areas

**The heart** of every LEGOLAND® Park is its unique MINILAND display. Constructed out of millions of bricks by the LEGOLAND Master Model Builders and populated by brick-built citizens, these constantly evolving and expanding 1:20-scale dioramas let visitors explore famous landmarks from their home countries and around the world, all in one amazing place ●

## BILLUND

At the original MINILAND in LEGOLAND® Billund, 20 million bricks have been used to create scenes of European life, with sections representing Denmark, Sweden, Germany, Norway, Finland and more. Passengers on the Miniboat ride sail past Thailand's Wat Phra Keo Temple, and Park guests can take in the entire amazing display from the top of a rotating panoramic tower.

## WINDSOR

Almost 40 million bricks went into building LEGOLAND® Windsor's MINILAND, which features city scenes from London and across Europe and the US, complete with traffic noises and moving cars, buses and trains. A newer addition is a space exploration section with a 1:20 scale version of America's Cape Canaveral and the John F. Kennedy Space Center.

**Famous London landmarks** at MINILAND UK include Canary Wharf, 30 St Mary's Axe, the Lloyd's Building, City Hall and the Millennium Bridge.

Copenhagen Nyhavn Harbour's red roofs are perfectly reproduced in LEGO® bricks.

**The largest part** of MINILAND Billund is the Port of Copenhagen, with moving miniature ships that travel 8,500 nautical miles a year.

## MALAYSIA

The centrepiece of the new LEGOLAND® Malaysia is its spectacular MINILAND display, which features scaled replicas of famous Asian towns and landscapes, assembled from over 25 million LEGO bricks with great care and detail.

**Motion technology** lets the people, animals, cars, ships, trains and aeroplanes of LEGOLAND Malaysia's MINILAND move at the touch of a button, together with location-appropriate background sounds.

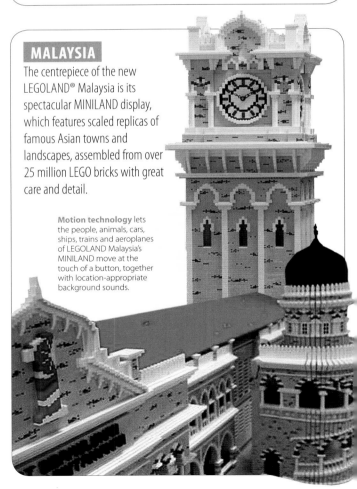

## GÜNZBURG

MINILAND at LEGOLAND® Deutschland includes miniature models of Berlin (like the Reichstag), the financial district of Frankfurt, a church and dairy from a Swabian village, Neuschwanstein Castle and Munich's famous airport and Allianz Arena. The Park's Venice display contains St Mark's Cathedral and the Doge's Palace, while canals, drawbridges and turning windmills adorn the Netherlands area. Attendees can interact with the 25-million-brick world by pressing buttons and moving joysticks to bring its intricate scenes to life.

An evening stroll in the Swiss city of Lucerne reveals glowing electric lights inside the miniature buildings and street lamps.

**Miniature divers** are captured in mid-leap (and mid-cannonball) at a Berlin swimming pool in MINILAND Deutschland. The swimmers and sunbathers may be plastic, but the water is real.

## FLORIDA

LEGOLAND® Florida's display, known as MINILAND USA, includes models of Daytona International Speedway; a pirate battle at Pirate Shores and sections of Florida, California, Las Vegas, Washington DC and New York City, with such sights as Times Square, the Empire State Building and the Bronx Zoo.

**The Capitol Building** and the Statue of Liberty together? Only at MINILAND USA!

## CARLSBAD

At LEGOLAND® California, mini-ice skaters enjoy a New York winter in Central Park, and New Orleans comes alive at Halloween with a cemetery filled with spooky skeletons. MINILAND Las Vegas has hotels, a wedding chapel and a working monorail, and giant miniature crowds gather on the steps of the Capitol Building in Washington DC every four years for the inauguration of the next President of the 23 million bricks of MINILAND.

**Watch out** for the moving cable cars! A LEGOLAND Master Model Builder works on a street scene in the MINILAND San Francisco display.

**500 photos** from every angle were taken to get the details of San Francisco's famous Steiner Street houses exactly right.

Realistically decorated gabled roof

Victorian clapboard architecture

# BEHIND THE SCENES OF *THE* LEGO® *MOVIE*

Matthew Ashton is Vice President of Design for Playthemes and Intellectual Properties at the LEGO Group. He is also an Executive Producer on *The LEGO® Movie*, and the creator of Unikitty. DK asked Matthew how *The LEGO Movie* came to life.

## What inspired the look of *The LEGO Movie*?

The directors were inspired by the visual style of the stop-motion videos created by our fan community, which can be found online. However, a feature-length stop-motion movie would take years and years to develop, and there probably wouldn't have been enough bricks on the entire planet (in the right colours) to get it done! So the stop-motion videos were used as a starting point, and we then imagined what kind of universe, characters and story could be created in the same style with an infinite number of LEGO bricks. The final movie animation was then created digitally, but made to look as close to traditional stop-motion animation as possible.

Matthew is based at the LEGO Group headquarters in Billund, Denmark.

Design Master Gitte Thorsen sculpts Vitruvius's wig, a LEGO piece that was created specifically for *The LEGO Movie*.

## How did the animations develop?

LEGO sculpting designers created new pieces for the movie, developing them in the same way they would for a real LEGO toy. Every component in the movie is a digital 3-D representation of a real LEGO brick; from the characters, buildings and locations to the visual effects, like bubbling lava, ocean waves and plumes of smoke! To achieve a realistic effect, the LEGO Group shipped bricks to the animation studio, Animal Logic. The studio looked at the pieces under a magnifying glass, and then resurfaced the digital files to make them look more authentic. If you look closely at the minifigure characters, you can see scratches, teeth-marks and fingerprints. Emmet even has grime in his leg holes, and Vitruvius looks like he has tumbled around in a toy box!

## How did you choose the LEGO locations?

There were many LEGO worlds and themes that we wanted to explore within *The LEGO Movie*, but they wouldn't all fit! Bricksburg had to be in there. It's where Emmet lives and the story begins, but it is also how many people imagine a LEGO world to be, from playing or building cities with their own LEGO bricks. An Old Western town seemed like a great location for a classic chase sequence. As Lord Business is set on stamping out creativity in the movie, we also needed a location that was the complete opposite to his vision – a world where creativity had no limits, and imaginations could run free – so Cloud Cuckoo Land was created for the movie as a colourful, creative, magical land where there are no rules.

## How did you develop the main characters?

They developed along with the story. As the story is very much centred around "building", the obvious job to give the main character, Emmet, was that of a construction worker. Wyldstyle was then created to be everything that Emmet wasn't: bold, confident, slick and streetwise, with mind-blowing building skills! We also couldn't make a LEGO movie without an iconic LEGO spaceman, complete with worn-away logo. A crack was added to Benny's LEGO helmet, since this was a common flaw with these helmets when they were first made. We worked extremely hard on MetalBeard, loading him up with every LEGO pirate ship icon we could think of, while making sure his size and movement were right for animation. Unikitty was the last of the gang to be created – we wanted her to be almost entirely brick-built to reflect her creativity.

Matthew and Michael Fuller work hard to keep track of the many minifigure characters in the movie.

Michael looks over some of the models he hand-built, including MetalBeard and Emmet's mech.

## How much of *The* LEGO *Movie* set was developed as real LEGO models?

Our focus from a LEGO perspective was to be highly involved in the development of the most prominent models seen in the movie, so we worked closely with the directors and animators to develop them as real models. The animation team was then entirely responsible for digitally creating all of the landscapes, crowds, buildings and background vehicles, based on the directors' briefings and taking inspiration from existing LEGO sets and artwork. Sometimes the directors had a very clear idea of what they wanted a key model to look like, and other times they came to the LEGO team for suggestions. Michael Fuller, Senior Product Designer at the LEGO Group, hand-built many of the key models from scratch. He had weekly video conferences with the film-makers, where amendments were suggested until the final LEGO model was realised. Some models, like Bad Cop's flying cop car, flew through the development process, while others, like MetalBeard, took a lot of refining!

Matthew and Concept Designer Matteo Oliverio finalise Unikitty's adorable design.

*The* LEGO *Movie* design team are real-life Master Builders.

# LEGO® Master Builders

Ridged grip for leverage

**Created in 1988,** the LEGO brick separator is a LEGO Master Builder's best friend. This simple, one-piece plastic tool can pop any brick off a model, no matter how tightly wedged-in it may be. A new orange version was released in 2012 that's compatible with LEGO Technic axles too.

Studs above and tubes below

**HAVE YOU EVER SEEN** a spectacular LEGO® sculpture and wondered who built it? Chances are, it was a team of LEGO Master Builders. Rigorously tested and selected for their creative construction skills, the LEGO Master Builders work at the LEGO model shops, where they assemble an incredible variety of models for in-store use, parks, special projects and events all around the world ●

The **Connecticut,** USA, model shop team assembles a 3.7m (12ft) long scale model of the newest LEGO factory in Monterrey, Mexico.

**LEGO Master Builders** can zoom in to make changes to individual bricks. Before digital building, they would have had to take apart the entire model first.

### DIGITAL BRICKS

The LEGO Master Builders once used half-scale prototypes to design their giant brick sculptures, but these days they use special computer programs to digitally create models before they start assembling the real thing.

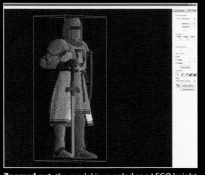

**Zoomed out,** the model is revealed as a LEGO knight. Purple highlights areas still being worked on.

### THE MODEL SHOP

Here's where the LEGO magic happens! With model shops in Denmark, the USA, the Czech Republic and at the LEGOLAND® Parks, the hard-working LEGO Master Builders are always in the middle of creating something new and amazing. Their workspaces are filled with LEGO models, giant building tables and racks of bricks in every shape, size and colour imaginable.

**LEGO Master Builders** love to use specialised pieces in unusual ways. Here, one works on a space monster made out of parts that started as a giant LEGO snake.

**A LEGO Master Builder** works near the prototype heads for a band of singing robots.

## LIGHT, SOUND & MOVEMENT

This 47,000-piece model of the Hollywood Bowl amphitheatre, built over the course of 600 hours for LEGOLAND® California's MINILAND, glows with rainbow-coloured electric lights that change to the beat of "The LEGO Symphony." Models with moving and light-up features are a specialty of the LEGO Master Builders.

## All built and ready for lift-off!

**A nose on a minifigure?** Built from about 2,400 bricks and standing 80cm (2.5ft) tall, these smiling characters are known as LEGO Friends.

Giant LEGO Friend version of a LEGO Mars Mission astronaut

## MASTER DESIGNS

Built at the Kladno model shop in the Czech Republic, this huge statue of an ancient Egyptian pharaoh was designed as a hand-drawn sketch and then constructed brick-by-virtual-brick in full scale on a computer before the first two plastic elements were ever snapped together.

## BUILT TO LAST

Models that will be placed on display outdoors must be sturdy and long-lasting. Some larger models are built hollow with a custom metal frame inside to support the weight of their thousands of bricks. Permanent models are usually glued together to make sure no birds or passers-by make off with stray pieces.

Mechanised moving jaw

**This animatronic** *Tyrannosaurus rex* head was built with an articulated, pneumatic metal framework inside that could automatically open and close its toothy jaws.

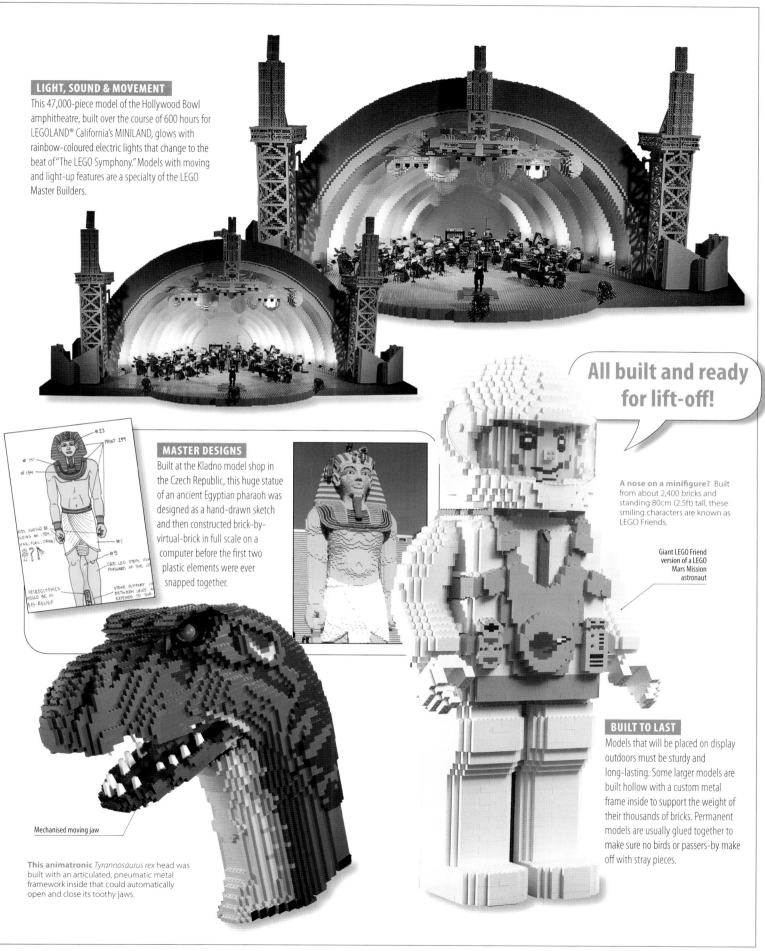

# LEGO® Brick Art

**SOME ARTISTS** paint on canvas. Others carve stone or weld metal. But a special few create art using the unique medium of LEGO® bricks and imagery. The work of these talented "Brick Artists" and others like them is a remarkable visual testament to the creative nature of LEGO building and the unlimited ways that it allows people to express themselves ●

**"Reflection"** (right) "is about seeing oneself in brick," Sawaya says. "As an artist, I tend to see the world in little rectangles, a lot like LEGO bricks."

"Red"
August 2005

"Reflection"
August 2006

## NATHAN SAWAYA

Brick artist Nathan Sawaya is a full-time freelance builder based in New York. His imaginative life-sized LEGO sculptures and giant mosaic portraits have been featured on television and in a North American touring museum exhibit titled "The Art of the Brick®."

## EGO LEONARD

In August 2007, a giant minifigure washed ashore on a beach in the Netherlands. Standing 2.5m (8ft) tall and carrying the enigmatic message "NO REAL THAN YOU ARE" on his shirt, the mysterious, ever-smiling Ego Leonard claimed to hail from a virtual world without rules or limitations, and to want to see "all the beautiful things that are there to admire and experience in your world."

**Newspapers and internet** blogs around the world marvelled at "the Giant LEGO Man" and wondered where he had come from.

**In November 2008**, the Dutch artist had an art show in, appropriately enough, the Brick Lane Gallery in London, England.

"Blue"
January 2006

"Yellow"
February 2006

## METAMORPHOSIS

Sinking into or emerging from a pile of bricks, opening up to reveal the inner nature, and even putting oneself together piece by piece, Nathan Sawaya's "Red", "Yellow" and "Blue" all represent transitions.
"I create art out of LEGO bricks to show people things they have never seen before, nor will they ever see anywhere else," the artist says.

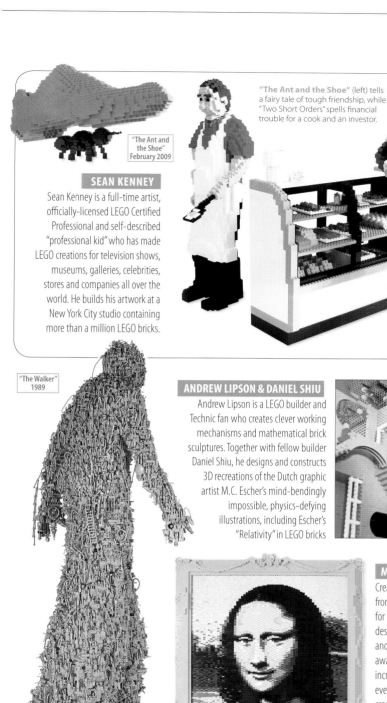

**"The Ant and the Shoe"** (left) tells a fairy tale of tough friendship, while "Two Short Orders" spells financial trouble for a cook and an investor.

"The Ant and the Shoe" February 2009

"Two Short Orders" October 2008

## SEAN KENNEY

Sean Kenney is a full-time artist, officially-licensed LEGO Certified Professional and self-described "professional kid" who has made LEGO creations for television shows, museums, galleries, celebrities, stores and companies all over the world. He builds his artwork at a New York City studio containing more than a million LEGO bricks.

"The Walker" 1989

## ANDREW LIPSON & DANIEL SHIU

Andrew Lipson is a LEGO builder and Technic fan who creates clever working mechanisms and mathematical brick sculptures. Together with fellow builder Daniel Shiu, he designs and constructs 3D recreations of the Dutch graphic artist M.C. Escher's mind-bendingly impossible, physics-defying illustrations, including Escher's "Relativity" in LEGO bricks

© A. Lipson 2003

## MOSAIC ART

Creating artistic mosaics and murals from LEGO bricks is a time-honoured hobby for many. Up close, the two-dimensional designs are clearly patterns of solid squares and rectangles, but as you move further away, the shapes and colours become increasingly real. LEGO mosaic artists use everything from scientific graph paper to cross-stitch needlework computer programs to turn photos and paintings into building blueprints.

**A LEGO mosaic** of the "Mona Lisa," Leonardo da Vinci's famous 16th century masterpiece, was created in 1993 to show how basic brick colours could be combined to create subtle shades.

## JØRN RØNNAU

Danish artist Jørn Rønnau grew up playing with the very first LEGO bricks. He describes "The Walker," which is made from 120,000 elements, as "an intuitive self-portrait... partly a robot, built from all kinds of special grey pieces, wheels, antennas, fire hoses, ladders, shovels etc. He can hardly move his feet... but he is surely trying!"

"Li" (2008)

## NICHOLAS FOO

Singapore-based artist Nicholas Foo is Asia's first LEGO Certified Professional. His Miniland-scale creation "Li," dedicated to the survivors of China's 2008 Sichuan earthquake, is made up of five small scenes that link together to form the Chinese character for strength and perseverance through adversity.

**"Li—Renewal":** planting a new beginning.

**"Li—Comfort":** care for the elderly.

**"Li—Rebuild":** the reconstruction of homes.

Curved roof design inspired by the builder's own covered cart model

# Fan Builders

**ALL OVER THE WORLD,** grown-ups are rediscovering their childhood love of LEGO® building – except for the ones who never lost it to begin with! With incredible talent and imagination, these AFOLs, or Adult Fans of LEGO, are pioneering new building techniques and detailing, attending fan groups and conventions and showing off their passion for the LEGO brick every day ●

BANK
Klocki-Zdroj

## SOLAR FLARE
Lino Martins, an AFOL from the US, built this bright and sunny classic 1960s station wagon in MINILAND scale for his LEGO car-builder group. It was displayed along with a friend's night-themed car and their Rockabilly band drivers at the Brickcon08 fan convention.

## THE BANK
Polish LEGO fan Paweł Michalak was inspired by the official Café Corner set to create his own model in the Modular Buildings style. "The Bank" was built for the LUGPol (LEGO User Group – Poland) "Klocki Zdrój" diorama.

**Nannan Zhang's** tiny, high-tech Yamamura Bike was built to race through the streets of a futuristic city.

## COLOGNE CATHEDRAL
Here's one dedicated AFOL! It took Jürgen Bramigk two long years to build this 3m (10ft) high model of Cologne Cathedral from his native Germany. Assembling it took about 900,000 LEGO bricks in different shades of grey.

**Maciej Karwowski** based his HD Bobber on the custom stripped-down motorcycles of the 1950s.

## DAY AT THE STABLES
Marcin Danielek's model of a two-storey country house with an attached horse stable includes details like a pile of chopped firewood, a dog chasing a cat up a tree and a clever use of LEGO pieces to let a skirt-wearing minifigure sit down.

### "CATCH UP!"

A 1955 San Francisco diner purchased by an eccentric billionaire and turned into a motorcycle and moped shop, this whimsical model was built by Jamie Spencer using custom decals and pieces from his LEGO City, LEGO Castle and LEGO® *Star Wars*™ collections.

Decals on model were custom-made by the builder

Roof recycled from Luna Unified School District, Bus No. 1

**Bill Ward** rebuilt this modern school bus out of his earlier model of a space-travelling bus of the future. The interior is full of misbehaving students and one very annoyed driver.

### NOPPINGEN

German fan Rainer Kaufmann grew up with the LEGO sets of the 1970s and rediscovered building almost 20 years later. His expansive Noppingen town display started as a one-man project, but has grown to include models made by his fellow builders.

Terrace overhang built from "log wall" pieces

**Rainer's Townhouse 3** model includes a sidewalk and section of street in front, and terraces overlooking a small yard at the back.

**Lemming** lives in the town of Noppingen. He loves walking, riding his bicycle, eating pizza and showing tourists around his hometown.

**Marvellous** old houses like these are common in Noppingen. Lemming's was completely renovated and looks like new.

**His favourite place** is the balcony of his second-floor flat. From there, he can look around and see the entire town.

### PICTURE STORIES

Many AFOLs like to build models that tell stories. Some are single-scene vignettes; others, like Rainer's "Lemming Presents his House" story, are created as a series of changing pictures.

# Fan-tasy & Sci-fi

**OFFICIAL LEGO® SETS** have to contain a fixed number of bricks, but there's no limit to the number of LEGO elements fan builders can use in their custom creations. Fan models can be as huge and as detailed as the builder desires. That really comes in handy when making other-worldly creations like spaceships and monsters ●

### THE TOWER OF BROTHERS

Once upon a time in a long-forgotten land, two brothers fought against each other in a crumbling tower. Maciej Karwowski's LEGO Castle fan contest-winning model is filled with spiral staircases, a hanging chandelier and an intricate use of small bricks to create an age-worn look.

**Maciej used** lots of small LEGO pieces to make his tower look like the site of an ancient battle.

Uneven stones from LEGO tiles

### GOLDFISH BALLOON

Wafting, drifting, swimming in the vast sky… Goldfish Balloon! Japanese builder Sachiko Akinaga has been building for more than 25 years and is known for her beautifully colourful and imaginative LEGO brick creations. Her portfolio of artistic models includes a car with a food-themed town hiding inside, an Earth Park with a motorised escalator and colour-changing fountain and a fortune-telling elephant.

Creeping vines

Ruined road

Membranes made from LEGO glider wings

### DRAGON FOREST

Bryce McGlone excels at using LEGO elements to create organic-looking shapes like robots and monsters. His Dragon Forest diorama, displayed at the BrickWorld 2007 LEGO fan convention, incorporates standard bricks with Technic parts to make a fierce mythical beast and rider.

## LL-X2 VANGUARD

Chris Giddens, the fan designer of the LEGO Factory Star Justice set, has his own style of retro-future sci-fi building that he calls "Pre Classic Space." Built in 2003, his LL-X2 Vanguard cruiser is a galactic peacekeeper starship with internal details that include an in-built fighter bay and a crew of bold space explorers.

Six heavy XLT deep space thrusters

In **Marcin Danielek**'s vertical "Double Trouble" vignette, a team of dwarven miners encounters unexpected surprises both above and beneath the ground.

Hungry cave worm

**Marcin Danielek's** "The Final Voyage" was the Medieval Journey winner in an online fan contest. Clever building techniques created the look of a half-submerged sea monster and floating debris and minifigures.

## STINGER LIGHT FIGHTER

This sleek starcraft was Australian fan Aaron Andrews's first LEGO spaceship model in more than 20 years. He built it with an opening cockpit, a female astronaut pilot and fold-down landing gear.

Building in solid or similar colours with elements of many different shapes and sizes can add realistic detail and complexity to a custom LEGO model.

Jointed arms with powerful claws

## INTERPLANETARY PROBE

Dan Rubin was inspired by the shapes of real-world insects when he built this biomechanical emissary of a mysterious alien race. Its sensitive grey internal mechanisms are protected by armour plating made from tan LEGO pieces.

## EXO-SUIT

Some MOC ("My Own Creation") makers like to specialise in a particular type of model, and UK builder Peter Reid's specialty is definitely his robots and "Neo-Classic Space" spacecraft. Unusual pieces and construction methods make his outer space exo-suit model really stand out in a crowd.

All-terrain legs

# Build It!

Here's an idea! Why don't you create some models that are so useful you won't ever want to break them up? LEGO® board games, pictures and small household items not only look great, they can have practical functions too.

Anyone for chess? This chess set looks cool and is perfect for a game of chess with a friend. Best of all, the pieces fit securely onto the board so you can even play it on the move! (See p.126)

# DESK TIDIES

Sort out your stationery with a LEGO desk tidy! Before you start, think about what you want to keep in your desk tidy: Pens, rulers, rubbers? Do you need drawers? How big should it be? A desk tidy should be practical and sturdy, but it can also brighten up a workspace, so add decoration in your favourite theme or colour scheme!

**BUILDING BRIEF**
**Objective:** Make desk tidies
**Use:** Workspace organisation, decoration
**Features:** Drawers, shelves, dividers
**Extras:** Secret compartments

## CASTLE DESK TIDY

This cool desk tidy has boxes for your pens and pencils, a drawer for smaller stationery – and it looks like a miniature castle! Start with the drawer and make sure it is big enough to fit whatever you want to store inside.

### STEP-BY-STEP

After you've built the drawer, make a box that fits neatly around it. Once the box is high enough to cover the drawer, top it off with some plates, adding decoration and open boxes.

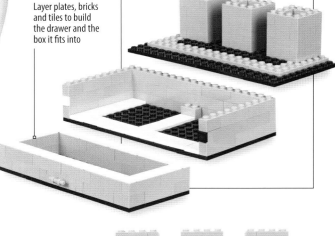

Layer plates, bricks and tiles to build the drawer and the box it fits into

**FRONT VIEW**

Need even more room for your stationery collection? Build boxes in various widths and heights

Simple, square open-topped boxes hold pencils and pens

Decorate your desk tidy with plates in contrasting colours

Grey, white and black bricks are good for a castle theme, but you can use any colours you want!

You could use a large plate to build the base of the drawer, but several small plates work if you reinforce them

Build a plate with handled bar into the drawer front so you can open it

# SEA MONSTER

Scare away stationery stealers with a sea monster desk tidy! Begin with a basic box shape, build in dividers, then add the features that make a monster of the deep. Can you think of other creatures that could keep your stationery safe? Have a go at making those too!

To make your sea monster even more frightening, add horns or fangs!

**FRONT VIEW**

A high, pointed tail can support bigger pens

Exposed studs on bricks create a scaly effect

Eyes made from 1x1 round plates inserted into headlight bricks

A red mouth adds detail and looks pretty scary!

Dividers can keep different kinds of stationery separate

BRING ME A NET TO CATCH THAT SEA MONSTER! THOSE PENS WILL BE MINE!

Sea monsters are mythical creatures, so no one really knows what they look like. What colour and shape will yours be?

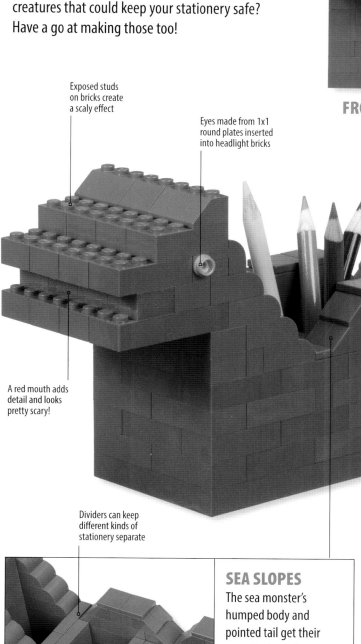

## SEA SLOPES

The sea monster's humped body and pointed tail get their smooth shape from slopes topped with tiles. You could also create humps by stacking bricks in stepped layers.

Curved bricks make a long, sloping neck

4x4 slope

**REAR SIDE VIEW**

# MINIFIGURE DISPLAY

Be proud of your minifigures! Show off your building skills by making a display stand to house your growing collection. You can add to your stand every time you get a new minifigure. You can even build stands in different styles to display minifigures from different LEGO themes!

**BUILDING BRIEF**
**Objective:** Build display stands
**Use:** Storage, decoration
**Features:** Sturdy enough to hold minifigures
**Extras:** Doors, moving parts

## DISPLAY STAND

You can make a display stand with simple bricks and plates. Build a basic structure that is stable and balanced. Then use special or interesting bricks to add detail. Choose exciting colours, or maybe use a colour that matches your bedroom. It's up to you!

**REAR VIEW**

### NEW HEIGHTS
A height of five bricks is tall enough to fit most minifigures nicely, but if yours has a large hat or helmet you may need to make the level higher.

You will know straight away if one of your figures is missing!

A mix of minifigures makes your display stand interesting to look at

Use pieces like curved half arches if you have them

Unusual shapes built with half arches. Inverted slopes would work too

Use plates, not tiles, so your figures can't fall off

Headlight bricks could hold tiles that correspond to minifigures

NOW'S MY CHANCE TO MAKE A RUN FOR IT!

Accessorise to match the theme of your stand. Add antennas or some droids!

## SPACE STATION DISPLAY

This space station stand is out of this world! White girders make this display stand look like something from outer space. If you decide to use fun and unusual bricks for your walls, make sure they're tall enough to house your minifigures!

Build the stand as wide as you need to contain all your minifigures

If you don't have a big enough plate, overlap smaller plates to whatever size you want

You could give your minifigures a control panel or an escape pod!

5...4...3...2...1... BLAST OFF! WHOA, WAIT FOR ME!

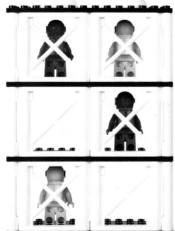

**REAR VIEW**

Girders come in a few LEGO® Town sets. Use any specialised bricks you have that fit your theme

## WORK IT OUT

How many minifigures do you want to display in your stand? Once you know, build each layer accordingly using pieces that fit your theme. These white girders look really space-age.

Choose colours to match your theme. For an underwater theme, use blue and green. What else can you think of?

If you don't have these pieces, try building with transparent bricks like windows – they look great as part of a space theme!

# BOXES

Are your LEGO pieces all over the place? Pencils scattered over your desk? These boxes are the answer. Think about what you will put in your box and how big it should be. It will need to be strong and stable to hold all your treasures. Choose a simple colour scheme and design – or just go crazy with your imagination. Don't feel boxed in!

**BUILDING BRIEF**
**Objective:** Make boxes to store your belongings
**Use:** Workspace organisation
**Features:** Hinges, drawers
**Extras:** Handles, dividers, secret drawers

**FRONT SIDE VIEW**

## SHINY BOX

This box will brighten up any desk – and make it tidy too! The bottom is made of large plates, and the sides are built up with interlocking bricks and topped with tiles for a smooth finish. The lid is built as a wall that is slightly larger than the top of the box.

A row of shiny tiles finishes off the box lid

Choose your favourite colours for your box

You could increase the height of your box so you have more room inside

NOT SURE THESE COLOURS ARE THE BEST FOR A GOOD NIGHT'S SLEEP!

### JOINTS THAT JOIN

The hinges are made from pairs of plates with bars and plates with horizontal clips. They are held in place by a row of tiles on top. To increase stability so you can use the box for longer, add more hinges.

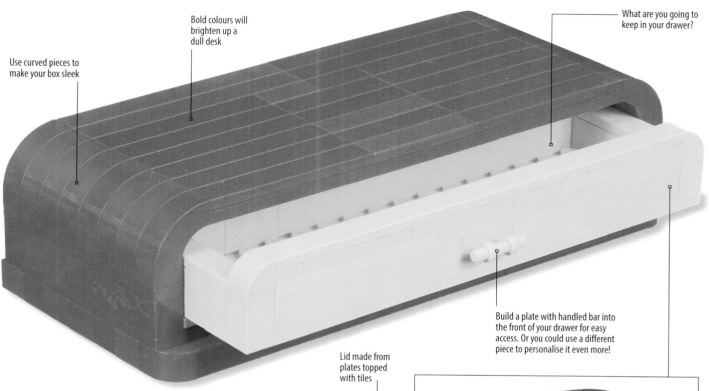

Use curved pieces to
make your box sleek

Bold colours will
brighten up a
dull desk

What are you going to
keep in your drawer?

Build a plate with handled bar into
the front of your drawer for easy
access. Or you could use a different
piece to personalise it even more!

## COOL CURVES

Boxes don't need to be boxy – they
can be curvy too! Use curved pieces to
create your desired shape. Make the
drawer first, then build the box around
it. Finally, create a base as a wall
turned on its side. Use bricks with side
studs to attach the base to the box.

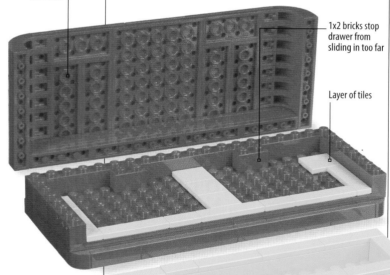

Lid made from
plates topped
with tiles

1x2 bricks stop
drawer from
sliding in too far

Layer of tiles

Curved half arch

**FRONT VIEW**

## SLIDING DRAWERS

To help the drawer slide easily, fix some tiles to the base
of the box. These will create a smooth layer so the
drawer won't catch on the studs as it slides in and out.

# CLASSIC BOARD GAMES

Classic board games can provide hours of fun. LEGO board games are no different – and they are ideal for long journeys because the pieces stay in place! All you need is a simple base and some game pieces. Don't know the rules? Ask your family or look online. You can even adapt the game to suit your favourite theme.

*FINALLY, IT'S MY CHANCE TO CAPTURE THE KING!*

## CHESS

A 16x16 base is a good size for lots of board games, including chess. If you don't have a baseplate, build one with overlapping plates to create a square. Then add eight rows of eight 2x2 plates in alternate colours to create a chessboard.

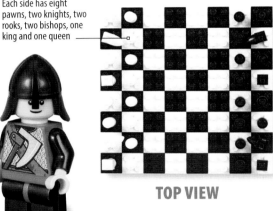

Each side has eight pawns, two knights, two rooks, two bishops, one king and one queen

**TOP VIEW**

A standard chessboard has black and white squares, but you can use any colours you want!

## CHECKMATE!

The chess pieces – pawns, knights, rooks, bishops, queens and kings –should be easy to distinguish. Will your queen have a big crown? Maybe your knight will have shining armour? Make sure the pieces are sturdy because they will be moved around a lot.

1x1 plate with vertical clip

Tooth plate for a horse's nose

Pawn

Bishop

Knight

King

Queen

Rook

Pawn    Bishop    Knight

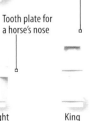
King    Queen    Rook

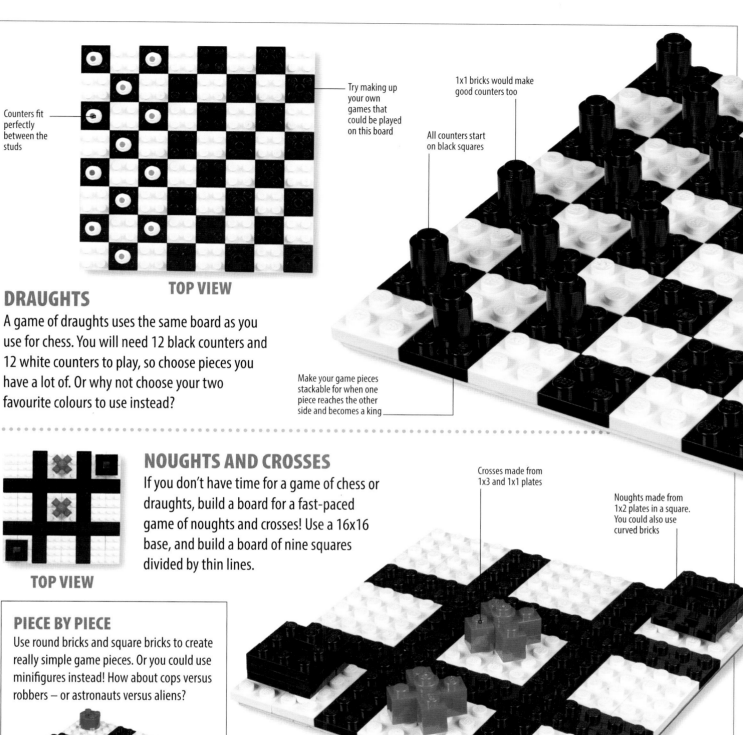

Counters fit perfectly between the studs

Try making up your own games that could be played on this board

1x1 bricks would make good counters too

All counters start on black squares

**TOP VIEW**

## DRAUGHTS

A game of draughts uses the same board as you use for chess. You will need 12 black counters and 12 white counters to play, so choose pieces you have a lot of. Or why not choose your two favourite colours to use instead?

Make your game pieces stackable for when one piece reaches the other side and becomes a king

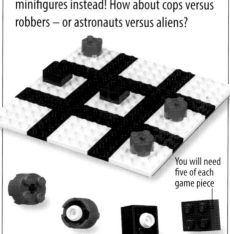

**TOP VIEW**

## NOUGHTS AND CROSSES

If you don't have time for a game of chess or draughts, build a board for a fast-paced game of noughts and crosses! Use a 16x16 base, and build a board of nine squares divided by thin lines.

Crosses made from 1x3 and 1x1 plates

Noughts made from 1x2 plates in a square. You could also use curved bricks

### PIECE BY PIECE

Use round bricks and square bricks to create really simple game pieces. Or you could use minifigures instead! How about cops versus robbers – or astronauts versus aliens?

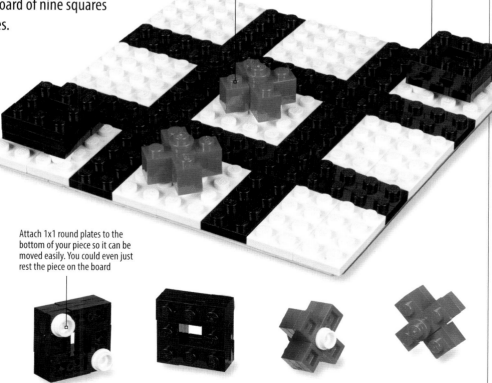

Attach 1x1 round plates to the bottom of your piece so it can be moved easily. You could even just rest the piece on the board

You will need five of each game piece

# Acknowledgements

**For the LEGO Group**
Head of the LEGO Idea House  Jette Orduna
Global Category Lead  Heike Bornhausen
Assistant Licensing Manager  Randi Kirsten Sørensen
Creative Publishing Manager  Paul Hansford

Writers  Hannah Dolan, Gregory Farshtey, Daniel Lipkowitz, Nevin Martell
Editorial Assistance  Beth Davies
Design Assistance  Richard Horsford

Photography
Joseph Pellegrino (pp.110-111), Ben Ellermann, Johannes Koehler, Yaron Dori (pp.50-51, pp.58-59),
Daniel Rubin (pp.54-55), Sarah Ashun (p.31), PHOTO: OOPSFOTOS.NL. (Mount Rushmore, p.18),
Steve Scott (Bilofix image, p.16), Gary Ombler, Thomas Baunsgaard Pedersen,
Brian Pulsen, Tim Trøjborg